A Case of Innocence

A Case of

by Douglas J. Keeling

A Birch Lane Press / Irma Heldman Book
PUBLISHED BY CAROL PUBLISHING GROUP

M

Kee ✓

A Birch Lane Press / Irma Heldman Book
Published by Carol Publishing Group

Editorial Offices
600 Madison Avenue
New York, NY 10022

Sales & Distribution Offices
120 Enterprise Avenue
Secaucus, NJ 07094

In Canada: Musson Book Company
A division of General Publishing Co. Limited
Don Mills, Ontario

Library of Congress Cataloging-in-Publication Data

Keeling, Douglas J.
    A case of innocence / by Douglas J. Keeling
      p.   cm.
    "Irma Heldman Book."
    ISBN 1-55972-007-7 : $15.95
    I. Title.
PS3561.E345C37   1989
813'.54--dc20   89-22086
                                                CIP

To Toni J., without whom . . .

A Case of Innocence

1

It was one of those afternoons when nothing you do seems right, one on which the air seems to hold a humid oppression that drapes itself over every action, thought, idea. People buy worthless stocks on days like this, lose badly at golf, commit suicide. I stared out the big windows of my office, chair swiveled around to face away from my desk, my feet propped up on the sill. I imagined that I could see tiny streaks of antipathy shooting through the air like billions of beta rays bombarding the city. The sky was gray and overcast yet not truly cloudy, the temperature was cool, but with a breath-warm feeling, and it was damp but not raining. A hollow, tepid kind of day.

I had been nosing through a file lying open across my knees that had occupied the same spot on my desk for a week, trying to decide whether Mrs. Sondham, now Ms. Baker, was going to pay me. Chances were slim. I'd gotten the divorce for her, but she'd lost custody of the kids, and that left her pretty unhappy. She'd gotten two drunk driving charges during the brief period that the divorce proceedings had been in progress. Jesus, no judge was going to let her keep the kids on a permanent basis. Drunk driving had really been under the hammer lately, and this lady seemed to have a problem. There had also been some evidence come out in the custody proceedings which indicated that Mrs. Sondham had become violent on occasion when she drank. Of course, she would blame my poor representation for the fact that she couldn't keep the kids. Nope, good ol' Mrs. Sondham, now Ms. Baker, would probably find better uses for that five-hundred dollars than to pay my fee with it.

It wasn't as if none of my clients paid. I was, after all, an officer of the court, attorney-at-law, defender of the downtrodden and all-around nice guy. Sure, if I nailed them for a retainer before letting them sit too long in my office, they were usually convinced of my admirable station in life and allowed me to keep it as payment in full for a job well done. Never mind that I had racked up three times that amount in time and expenses. Maybe that's what motivated me to diversify into a parallel line of work. Or maybe I just got tired of paying out-of-pocket expenses to some other clown calling himself a private investigator who would take three weeks to track down some guy who was several months behind on his child support. Let's not even consider the fact that the guy is right here in town the whole time. Much faster, easier and cheaper to do it myself, so why not have the appropriate license? No, it probably wasn't the expensive incompetence of the other bozos that motivated me. I probably just needed an excuse to carry a gun. I wallowed in my sarcasm and foul thoughts as I examined the gray-brown dirt in the creases and serrated seams of my worn cordovan wing tips. I couldn't remember the last time I'd had them polished. Waste of time, anyway. Shoes get dirty too easily, down there close to the grit and pavement. Theirs is a dirty business.

I watched out the window as a city bus with ugly green and blue stripes painted across the side stopped and swung its folding doors open. My imagination provided the familiar hydraulic hissing that always accompanies the sight. The bus picked up an elderly woman waiting on the corner, and then pulled away from the curb leaving a plume of dark diesel smoke behind. My olfactory nerve endings reacted to the imagined acrid smell of the diesel exhaust. My office seemed to be filled with it. Maybe it was just the stale aroma of too much steam heat in the old building.

Okay, so it was a Thursday afternoon and I was a bit grouchy. After chewing on a paper clip and staring out the window for a while longer, I wandered out into the reception area and told Janette she could take off early.

"What the hell," I said, "we don't have anybody to sue today anyway."

"Well, if that's the deciding factor, I could leave early every day," Janette said wryly.

"Don't forget who signs your paycheck," I said.

"I do," she reminded me.

"Oh yeah." It's hell working with a liberated woman.

Janette packed up and left while I went back to my window-gazing. It wasn't really that I didn't have anywhere to go, it was just my office policy. We always had someone at the ready, manning the phones, at least until five. True, I was in no big hurry to leave. Home had been a depressing place lately. Actually, everywhere had been depressing of late, but the feeling seemed to be more acute inside my little two-bedroom house in the middle of its working-class neighborhood full of kids, dogs and women in jogging suits. Maybe it was just being alone among others who weren't. Whatever it was, it was gnawing away at me the way water erodes hard soil, and I could feel little bits of my normally glib persona slipping away with the tide of ambivalence that had been tugging at me for several weeks. A more literary sort would call it a blue funk. I called it the shits.

The phone rang twice before I swung around in my chair and picked it up. I could hear faint sobbing sounds on the other end. I said "Hello" in what was probably not a very pleasant tone.

"Mister Casey?" came the soft voice finally, between sniffles.

"This is he," I replied. "What can I do for you?" Business-like and polite.

"I need to see you right away," said the voice, now gaining strength.

"I'll be here until five, can you make it by then?"

"Yes."

"Do you know where my office is?"

"Yes." She hung up.

That wasn't a strange phone conversation in my office. The door reads: "James P. Casey, Attorney at Law," and down lower on the same pane of frosted glass: "Private Investigator." Either shingle generates its share of calls like this one. The heartsick mother whose teenage daughter has taken off for New York City, the young housewife who's just been served with the divorce petition, or the battered young girl desperate to get away from her stepfather. They all sound about the same on the phone, and an inordinate number of them seem to end up on the line with me.

When she didn't show by 5:15, I got my jacket and gun out of the closet and locked up the office. I clipped the gun holster to the left side of my belt as I walked down the hallway. You never know when you'll run into opposing counsel.

As I got to the bottom of the stairs, I saw her rush in the door to the building and stare back out across the parking lot as the door swung shut. She had to be my caller, her eyes were red and puffy and she had the look of a frightened puppy. She wore a heavy wool coat with the collar turned up and a fuzzy red scarf tied around the outside of the lapels. Since it wasn't all that cold outside, the get-up was probably supposed to make her less recognizable. Her shoes left gummy footprints the color of the light mud from the gravel parking lot on the tile floor of the entryway. Her shoes were dirtier than mine.

"I'm James Casey," I said.

"Oh, I'm sorry," she said, turning quickly, "you scared me. I'm..." she glanced back at the door, "I'm sorry I'm late, but I thought somebody was following me."

"Well," I said, "the office is closed up and they don't trust me with a key, so if you want to talk you'll have to ride along to the Burger King down the street and fill me in on your problem while I enjoy the cuisine." I smiled. My charm was being wasted on her. She wasn't paying attention.

We got into my car and headed east on Douglas Avenue. The Burger King was actually about a half mile down and a couple blocks over, but I didn't get the feeling she would notice.

The sky had turned a dull, dark gray, and about half the cars on the road had their headlights turned on. The other half were washed-out, colorless shapes in varying shades of gray or brown that moved without flash or sparkle against a monotone backdrop that all but absorbed them. Driving can be treacherous that time of day, that time of year. November in Kansas generally has very few sunsets, just dim afternoons that fade into colorless dusks and then hazy black nights. The lights just sort of slowly go out.

"Why don't you start out by telling me your name and then tell me why you think someone would be following you."

"I'm ... well, that's not that easy, I mean, my name is Linda Matasseren and my ex-husband is, he's ..." Her sentence trailed off into silence.

"Well, we've made some progress," I said, "we know that you've gotten the divorce out of the way already." I was not winning her over with my sense of humor. She sat huddled against the door, staring at me blankly. Let's correct that. I've seen blank stares in my time, and this one was way beyond that. Let's call it a vacant stare, vacant of consciousness or reality. She wasn't even aware of what I'd said. I was looking at a ceramic mask with two dark holes for eyes.

"Okay, let's get serious for a minute," I said. "I get the feeling that you're not coming to see me about a divorce or child custody case. If it's about a missing person, you must be it, because you seem more concerned about someone finding you than you locating someone else. Why don't you just try to relax and tell me what the problem is." I pulled into the Burger King and parked.

"It's my daughter," she blurted out. "It's Sara and they've taken her and Paul thinks I know where his stash is and so do they. Oh my God, they'll kill her. I don't know where his stash is. They'll kill her."

It all came out like a dam bursting. I swear she told the whole thing in not more than three breaths.

It seemed that Paul was her ex-husband and a small-time but ambitious drug dealer. He'd smuggled a small fortune in cocaine into the country from South America and was in the process of distributing it here in the States under the cover of some sort of sporting goods operation. The merchandise was supposedly stashed here in Wichita while awaiting the next step of the distribution scheme. He had evidently figured that this would be a good hub out of which to run a supply operation for the entire Midwest. The state and federal drug enforcement agencies caught wind of Paul's deal and had planted a bust, but it went sour and they nailed him holding only a couple of sample snootfuls. Of course, they were after the Mother Lode, but Paul wasn't telling any of his secrets. Paul didn't seem to be one for telling very many secrets to anyone, because his partners in the setup, a dealer from Dallas and the sporting goods connection from Kansas City according to what Linda knew, didn't have a clue as to where he'd stashed the coke either.

Paul got word to his partners that unless and until he got out of his fix with the law enforcement officials, no one was going near the stuff. His partners went asking the ex-wife about the location of their merchandise and she seemingly played dumb. In reality, at least from what she was telling me, she had never been privy to the hidey-hole and didn't have a clue as to where the drugs were. The partners snatched the six-year-old daughter and informed mom and dad that she'd be staying with them until somebody could come up with the whereabouts of the dope. Paul remained silent and Linda didn't know where the stuff was. Little Sara was the pawn. This had all taken place two days ago and

Linda had since been begging Paul to tell her where to find the stash for the sake of their child. He felt strongly about his priorities, and he didn't see himself as a family man. Linda had gotten my name from an ex-client who thought I wore blue tights and a red cape under my lawyer's garb, and had come to me in desperation as she grew more concerned over Sara's well-being. She knew she couldn't go to the police or Sara would be as good as dead. And to think, an hour and a half ago I was fretting over Mrs. Sondham's, now Ms. Baker's, unpaid invoice. Life certainly has it's crescendos and pianos.

2

I had ordered a burger, fries and a Coke from the Drive-thru and was eating them back at my office. Linda, having sullenly declined my offer to treat her to similar fare, now stared silently across my desk at me as I ate my dinner. She was curled up sideways in my client chair with her legs tucked up under her butt and her head resting against the soft wing. It was an overstuffed wing-back, covered in worn red leather, good for just such a posture. I'd picked it up at an estate sale right after I started out on my own and had kept it through two different office locations and as many desks. I always kept it positioned directly in front of my desk, back to the door. It is the sort of chair that seems to give clients a quiet reassurance that they are being well taken care of. It fosters confidence, privacy and anonymity; anyone sitting in it is invisible from almost any angle but straight on. I have this fantasy that no one seated in that chair can lie to me, but experience has shown that to be untrue. Still, I continue to believe. Hope springs eternal.

Linda Matasseren looked to be about twenty-seven. She was reasonably attractive in an angular sort of way, with a hard, sharp jaw and bright dark eyes. Her narrow nose was set prominently between high, sharp cheekbones. The straight jawline ran far back below her ear and turned abruptly down into a strong, slender neck. She wore her dark red hair in a short kind of punkish style, with an unnecessary little whirl in front that hung down low over her left eyebrow. Her purple hose covered shapely but slightly thick legs and the purple leather skirt was consistent with the hairdo. I thought that she would do better trying to look her age rather than ten years younger. Of course, she hadn't come to me for a fashion consultation.

I finished my food and wadded up the paper wrappers and boxes in which it had been packaged. The crackling of the paper made a tremendous amount of noise in the otherwise silent office. I stood up and took off my jacket. I saw her eyes get big and focused as I unclipped my gun and slid it into a drawer.

"I've got a permit," I said nonchalantly. I tossed my trash into a wastebasket beside the desk.

"Oh," she said. Maybe she'd overextended herself back in the car. She pulled nervously back and forth on a gold nugget charm which hung from a gold chain around her neck as she stared into the front of my desk. Her lower lip worked itself in and out as she chewed on the inside of it. Every once in a while she would lift the gold nugget to her mouth and run her tongue across the edge. I settled back into my chair, drank my Coke and watched her fidget. She wore no rings at all on either hand, wedding or otherwise.

"Explain to me please, Mrs. Matasseren, exactly what it is that you want me to do for you."

"I'm not really sure," she said. "When I got your name from Danny Curl, he said you could help. He said you could help when maybe nobody else could. He said you could find Sara and bring her back safe." Nothing like a big buildup.

"The first thing that you have to realize is that kidnapping involves the federal people. The drug operation already seems to have aroused a lot of interest from the law enforcement folks, and the people who have Sara are after the same thing the cops are. And then there's just little ol' me over here on the sideline and I'm supposed to pull an end run on them all. I don't think the situation is even realistic."

"But I don't have any other..."

"Wait," I interrupted firmly, "I'm not finished. I've also got this obligation to inform those nice law enforcement people and the courts of any crimes that have been committed and

take steps necessary to prevent any further crimes from ensu-
ing. I don't see any way that I can help you without blatantly
turning my back on all that."

"I don't give a shit what you do," she said with sudden
harshness. "I've got to get Sara back alive, and if you can't
help me, I've got to find someone who can."

She picked her purse up off the floor and dug around for a
couple of seconds, coming out with a snapshot, which she
slid across the desk at me.

"That's Sara."

Jesus, just like in the movies. I'm supposed to be overcome
with emotion at the sight of this helpless child and say: "All
right, I'll help you. Damn the consequences." Unfortunately,
real life doesn't work that way. I had a living to make, licenses
to be concerned about losing and years to be concerned
about spending as a free man. I'd be the first to admit that
I'm a sucker for a cause and a champion of the underdog, but
super-moral movie heroes are a far cry from an everyday guy
like me. I eat dry cereal out of a plastic cup on my way to the
office in the morning. I have holes in almost every pair of
socks I own. I mow my own yard, and I sweat when I do it. I
looked at the picture for a good long minute.

"All right," I suddenly heard my voice saying to Linda
Matasseren, "I'll help you. Damn the consequences."

I spent the rest of the evening gathering as much information as I could from Linda about her ex-husband, his drug
business, his contacts and anything else that occurred to me
as even slightly important. The more we talked, the more
animated and intense she became. With the animation came
a more fully developed personality and an observable beauty
that the surface alone did not reveal. The hard angular lines
became clean, smooth profiles. The awkward thicknesses
were transformed into a soft, rich fullness. I was beginning to
like her.

She didn't want to go back to her house, saying that she
was sure that it was being watched, so I called Janette and

asked her if she could take on a boarder. This wasn't the first time I'd asked the favor, in fact it was a fairly usual occurrence. A stream of battered wives and children, runaway teenagers and scared pregnant girls without husbands had found their way from my chair to Janette's big old house on a fairly regular basis. Janette's education and training had been as a social worker before she came to work for me, but I had yet to find something that she couldn't do, and do well. Legal secretary, counselor, arbitrator and security guard, she could wear quite a few hats. Her parents had been killed in an airplane crash when she was in college, and she was left with a big old two-story house in a nice part of town. There were plenty of beds, the rent was right and she hadn't complained yet. In addition to the house, Janette had been the sole beneficiary of a substantial hunk of life insurance, the proceeds of which were in a trust. She was pretty well set, and really didn't need to work at all, but that didn't stop her from bitching occasionally about the lousy wages I paid her.

Janette is a wisp of a blonde, the kind that gets swept up and carried away by the hero in movies. Her skin is so fair that it's almost pasty, but on her it comes off as a milky glow. Her pale blue eyes neither sparkle nor dance, but they are so large and sincere that most people find it difficult to deny her anything that she truly wants. A tiny point of a nose and rich, full lips round out a look that was meant for the big screen during the 1940s. All in all, she is not beautiful. She is simply and undeniably pretty, no more, no less. She elicits comments from almost every client who comes into the office, male or female. Often, in fact, the male clients spend more of their visit out front chatting with Janette than they do in my office discussing business with me. Maybe I should start billing them for the time they spend with her. They would probably pay.

The feature that keeps the clients hanging around is not one that can be discovered upon visual inspection. It becomes evident when Janette opens her mouth and speaks, directing her attention and focusing those soft blue eyes on you. She can give a total stranger the feeling of complete and instant familiarity. For the time that she gives you, she is totally yours, all the energy of her attention is focused directly on you. There is no one else in the room, the building, the world. You become the center of the universe. It is a powerful gift. I often tease her saying she should have been a TV evangelist or a high-priced call girl. Only the most talented and successful in those callings share her rare ability.

Beneath all of this soft, spellbinding presence, however, is the Janette that I love and respect. A tough, gutsy, thoroughly ruthless and totally focused predatory she-animal that would fight to the death to defend honor, family or employer. Fiercely loyal, amazingly capable and unquestioningly direct; as good a right hand as anyone could ask for.

If she ever really made a demand for more money, I'd have no choice but to cough it up. I'd be lost without her. Maybe someday she'd adopt me.

I drove Linda over to Janette's. Mark Glennings, Janette's boyfriend, rode back with me to pick up Linda's car. I had never figured out why those two didn't get married. They had dated since before I hired Janette, and that had been almost five years ago. Maybe they had seen what a mess I'd made of a marriage and decided not to follow a bad example. Probably smart.

The next morning, I headed out to the courthouse, briefcase in hand, attired in my best gray wool lawyer's costume, complete with red silk tie and a fresh white shirt. Never let anyone say that I can't look the part if I try.

I had a hearing scheduled on a motion to modify support payments in a divorce that had been nothing but a grudge match from the very beginning. As I hurried in the back door of the courthouse, right next to the sheriff's department, I spied Jay Price kneeling beside what I figured was probably his client. Jay was making his point with the young black man in the best lawyerly fashion, but the guy's eyes were glazed over and he was rocking slowly back and forth, staring at a point which must have been behind and above Jay's head, his hands clenched between his knees. The metal bench on which he was seated creaked each time he shifted his weight. Jay didn't seem to notice that he'd been tuned out.

Jay is something of a memorable vision. He looks like a Dennis the Menace who's been overdosed on growth hormones. His permanently unkempt sandy-blond hair and freckled face are those of a mischievous eight-year-old. His six-foot-eight-inch frame makes him tower above almost any crowd. These features, combined with the almost comical way his sleeves and pantlegs never quite reach the proper places along his exaggerated, bony limbs, make him a sight that is difficult to avoid staring at, and very hard to forget.

"Morning, counselor," I said. "It would appear that your advice falls on deaf ears."

"Hi, Case," Jay said, standing up. He always makes me feel incredibly short when he's standing within twenty feet of me. "I'm about ready to plead this guy as insane. Jeez, he's busted on a marijuana charge two days ago, and he's stoned out of his head when I come up here to plead him today."

"Dedication," I said. "Listen, I've got some files I'd like you to baby-sit for the next week or so if you've got time. A couple of domestic hearings and a DUI sentencing. Mostly hand-holding stuff. Do you mind?"

"Ah-ha, Sir Lancelot is at it again," he said with a grin and a sigh. "When are you going to learn that you'll never get ahead playing knight errant while someone else works all your cases?"

"The problem, Jay, is that you assume I want to get ahead. I'm not even sure what it is that I'm supposed to be getting ahead of. Janette can give you the files and fill you in on the details if you'll call her this morning." I turned and headed down the corridor. "Thanks a ton, Jay," I called back over my shoulder.

"No problem, Case," I heard him say from around the corner. "Good luck."

I knew what Jay was thinking. Poor Case, that dumb son of a bitch never got his head screwed on straight, forever destined to be an oddball. Jay and I first met in law school. We were both the type who chose to sit at the back of the classroom, and we had enough classes together that we eventually got to know each other pretty well. We spent a lot of time studying and relaxing together, and discovered that we shared a cynical, sideways view of the world and its inhabitants. Jay went through a small crisis after graduation, right before we took the bar exam and, without patting myself on the back, I pulled him through it. He even passed the bar, first try. He'd also gotten very attached to my now ex-wife Annie during that period, so all three of us were happy when both Jay and I took jobs in Wichita.

As it turned out, Jay ended up being much happier than Annie and me. The emotional dependence on her that he'd developed became a real burden, sort of like having the child that wouldn't grow up and leave home. Annie became his mother-figure, and the relationship added a real strange twist to the marital strain between Annie and me that eventually led to our divorce. After Annie and I split up, though, the tension eased and both of us managed to remain good friends with Jay. Both Jay and I were on our own now, sole practitioners. Although we trusted each other implicitly, we had never discussed a partnership. I think we both liked the arrangement the way it was. I'd go off on some fool project, leaving Jay to pick up my slack, and he would shovel a lot of work my way that he found "unsavory." Lots of the clients even thought that we were partners. The arrangement worked well.

My hearing took about an hour and a half. I was in the office by 10:15.

"Jay Price called and I got him squared away," Janette said as I came through the door. "Linda Matasseren is still at my house, Judge Rogers' clerk wants to know if you're going to submit a pretrial in the Garlington case, and Mark wants to know if he gets paid for his taxi service."

"It was actually auto-ferrying, not taxi service," I said. "Tell him if he's a good boy, I'll give you next week off so he can get to know you better."

"He'll be thrilled," she said.

I put my briefcase and coat in the closet and went into the small bathroom that adjoins my office to change clothes. I hung my suit, tie and shirt carefully from a hanger on the back of the door. You never know when you'll need to spiff up. I pulled an only slightly dirty and very worn pair of tan cords and a green, flannel shirt from the cabinet beneath the sink and sighed in relief as I put them on. I definitely prefer the uniform of the private investigator to that of the lawyer. I glanced into the mirror and smiled at myself. The flannel shirt I'd donned had tan corduroy patches on the elbows and on the front of the right shoulder. A shooting shirt. Or was it a hunting shirt? Whatever it was called, it was well-worn and comfortable. And stylish, in an outdoorsy sort of way.

"You probably figured out from what Jay told you that I'm going to be hitting this Matasseren thing for the next couple of weeks," I said as I stepped back into Janette's outer office. "You can do whatever needs to be done to hold down the fort, then you're on your own. Pitch anything that needs special attention at Jay."

"Standard procedure," Janette said without looking up from the stack of mail she was sorting through.

I went back into my office and poked at the plants. An unusually bright sun shone in warmly through the big southern-exposure windows behind my desk.

"Drink up, fellas," I said to the plants, "you won't get much of this kind of sunshine during the wintertime in Kansas."

The enormous windows letting all that natural sunlight spill in had probably been the main reason I had taken the office. The fact that the rent was right had a lot to do with it, too. It was in an old commercial building just out of the downtown area that had been remodeled a few years ago to house retail space on the front side, along Douglas Avenue, with two stories of office space and parking on the back side. I was on the second floor, at the south end. From those windows behind my desk you could see a slice of the world at street level through a ten-foot space between the two red brick walls that formed my building and the one next door. Visible through that ten-foot space was a street corner, the intersection of Douglas and Grove, a bus stop, a piece of the frontage of a music store and, off in the distance, the campus, parking lot and a wall full of windows belonging to Wichita East High School. In warm weather there would be students lounging and playing in the green grass in front of the school building during the lunch hour. Whenever I began to feel caged or restless, I would seek the solace of that ten feet of escape and activity, my airshaft to reality.

None of the offices in the building could be characterized as luxurious or modern by any stretch of the imagination, but the big paned windows in my office had wisely been left undisturbed by the remodeling, and maintained the stately presence they had been designed for when the building was constructed in the early 1940s. The outer office housed Janette and her equipment fairly well, but there wasn't much room left as a reception area. That was all right, we didn't do much receiving, just shuffling through. My office was a little bit larger and had pale green walls. Janette described them as "hospital green." I had never painted them because I thought the color contributed to the charm of the place. Janette said that they were ugly, an embarrassment, and that she was going to have them painted sometime when I was out of town. She was probably right, and she probably would.

Most of the furniture in the two rooms was second-hand, but it seemed to be in keeping with the rest of the decor. An odd-lot of liquidation sale office furniture and discarded household items served us well. What pulled it all together were the plants. I'd gotten on a plant-growing kick a couple of years ago during a period when business was especially slow, and now they dominated the otherwise unoccupied areas of the office. Spreading philodendrons covered the shelves, alcoves and window ledges while areca palms, rubber plants and ficus trees laid claim to the corners and spaces between furniture. Janette and I were supposed to share the duties of care, but most of the time she did the feeding and maintenance while I provided moral support. It worked out nicely.

I grabbed a dark brown corduroy jacket from a hook on the back of my office door, retrieved my gun from the drawer of my desk and clipped the holster to the waistband of my pants. I avoid belts when possible, they tend to be irritating on the underside of a solid but slightly protruding stomach like mine.

"Is it all right if Linda stays with you until I get this thing worked out for her?" I asked Janette on my way out.

"Do I have any choice?" she asked, flashing me a glimpse of the smile that can work miracles; soothe the savage client, explain away missed deadlines and make a heavy fee seem tolerable. In fact, I consider that smile so formidable a weapon that Janette has been instructed to use it on me only in dire circumstances. She must have let that one slip.

"Sure," she conceded after letting me squirm for a few seconds, "as long as all of the furniture is still there when I get home tonight."

"Thanks," I said, starting out the door, "you're a peach."

"What about Garlington and your 3:00 today with Mr. Feldt?"

"Tell Judge Rogers' clerk 'yes' on Garlington, but it probably won't be until the week of the filing deadline. Call Feldt and tell him we can put it off until next month, it's just some corporate stuff. That should be no problem. Reschedule a time and date if you can.

"Be careful," she said quietly as I shut the door.

3

Wichita, Kansas, is not a particularly large city, although it is the largest one in the state. Most people don't realize that the biggest portion of Kansas City lies in the state of Missouri, so Wichita is the largest by default. The population of the Wichita metro area hovers around the three-hundred thousand mark. The aircraft industry, in its strange feast-or-famine production cycles that seem to run almost opposite most other industries or economic indicators, keeps the economy a bit above the national trend, and the cost of living is very palatable in comparison to other cities of similar size across the country.

There are quite a few large business interests which call Wichita their home or have their roots here. The general public, however, is seldom aware of this fact, or it is an item of trivia that doesn't register much interest. Who knows or remembers that the Carney brothers sold their first Pizza Hut pizza from a small Wichita home in the 1950s? Bill Lear, a Wichitan by choice, rose to great heights with his LearJet and the eight-track tape. A.A. Hyde developed Mentholatum Lip Balm here in the 1890s. Koch Industries, a Wichita-based company, is one of the ten largest privately-held corporations in the world. The Coleman Company supplies the world with lanterns and other outdoor equipment from its Wichita home plant. McConnell Air Force Base, once host to a cluster of Titan II Missiles, is now one of the designated bases for the B-1B Bomber.

There always seems to be a lot of money flowing through the city, and it serves as kind of an exchange point for some very diverse big-business interests. Much of the money stays here, a portion of it stays only briefly and some of it goes away forever. By and large, though, Wichita holds a bigger stick in the financial and socio-political circles than most people, including the residents, realize.

On this particular day, however, those otherwise attractive attributes were a bit abrasive to my particular purposes. Finding a kidnapped girl in a city this size would be hard enough without the ease and speed at which she could be moved along any one of those constantly flowing conduits of money, information and goods upon which our economy thrives. Also, knowing that we had people from Kansas City and as far away as Dallas involved, and the obvious enormity of the problems that could create, made me very nervous. Nevertheless, I was optimistic.

The brilliant sunlight danced off the windshields of the cars in the parking lot of my building. Barely visible wisps of steam rose off of the frost-whitened clumps of grass that lined the edge of the lot. The building cast a cold blue shadow diagonally across the row of hoods on the automobiles parked along the sidewalk, and stretched out to engulf the two small trees growing at the end of the sidewalk that struggled to grow each spring, only to be bent back by each winter's harsh dose of foul weather. The trees looked like two timid animals, huddled precariously at the end of the long shadow. I could almost see them shiver. I got into my sun-warmed car and headed out to try to tap my first source of information.

Mike Ahearn had been a friend of mine since our high school days here in Wichita. In fact, we'd played some football together until my knees became wiser than the rest of my body and convinced me that there were some more enduring and less painful pursuits in life. Mike had always been something of a maverick, doing pretty much his own thing, but managing to fit into the flow of things when it became important to him. In other words, he could play the game when he had to. It turned out to be a good thing for him to be able to do. He became a cop after a short hitch in the Army and spent a couple of years on the street, a few behind a desk and finally ended up where he'd wanted to be all along, in the Plainclothes Narcotics Detective Division. I figured that he would be a good place to start picking up leads and information on a drug-related case. Our relationship went back far enough and we'd had enough common ground in our work that I knew I could at least get a general briefing on the Matasseren situation from the official point of view, if Mike knew anything about it, without the need for a lot of explanation and dealing with sticky questions.

I knew that I would probably not be able to find Mike directly, since he worked undercover most of the time, and that any message I would leave with the police department might take a week to find its way to him. I could usually locate him fairly quickly through his wife Marcia, so I tried her first.

Marcia worked in the public relations/marketing department of one of the local hospitals. I pulled into the emergency parking lot and went in through the emergency entrance. I walked past a battery of nurses behind a glassed-in station and a gleaming white admissions counter like I belonged there, and I was on the second floor administrative office wing in no time at all. When in doubt, act like you know what you're doing. Marcia Ahearn was not at her desk, but the receptionist told me that if I would take a seat she would find her for me. Hospitals make me nervous. I have spent too many unpleasant hours as an involuntary visitor to ever allow me to be totally at ease with being there on my own volition. This particular hospital was better than most. There was an abundance of dark red brick used throughout the interior, deep beige carpeting and coordinated beige-and-rust tweed fabric furniture. The feel was very different from the bright, sterile chrome-and-light atmosphere found in most hospitals. I waited in comfort and without anxiety, looking at a copy of *Fortune* magazine. Appropriate for the business end of a hospital.

"Case?" I heard Marcia's voice call from across the waiting area.

"Hi, Marcia," I said, rising. "How's this fine day holding together for one of my favorite ladies in this hospital?" I noted that her sleek black hair and dark eyes still set off her brilliant smile as nicely as I had remembered. There were a few lines around her eyes and mouth that had appeared since the last time I had seen her, but they looked good on her. She was compacted into a snug-fitting dark skirt and a silky dark maroon blouse with padded shoulders which emphasized her tiny but slightly robust figure. Conservative but provocative.

"So far, so good, I guess," she said, blushing slightly. She had a worried and inquiring look on her face. "You're not here about Mike are you?"

"Yeah," I said, quickly motioning with both palms toward her, "but don't worry. I just need to know how to get in touch with him."

"Oh," she breathed out with relief, "it always scares me when someone comes asking about him. Ever since he started working undercover... you know." She had raised her small hand to her throat and was patting her fingers lightly against the top of her sternum. Although she had relaxed visibly, her breath still came in short bursts, her chest heaving with the effort. The diamond in her wedding ring sparkled in the dim light with each movement.

"I know," I said sympathetically. It still bothered me every time I was reminded of the kind of constant fear people live in when the fates dictate that they love someone who does dangerous work. I had imposed that kind of smothering dread on someone before, and she couldn't take it. It made matters worse that I had been unable or unwilling to leave the work for her. She had no choice but to leave me.

"He's been up in Newton the last three weeks or so. He's staying somewhere up there, I think he must be setting up some sort of bust on a local dealer or something. You know how he is about keeping that stuff to himself." She looked up at me briefly. "He's only home on some weekends, and I know he won't be here this one, but if I need to get in touch with him I'm to leave word with a Sergeant Collins at the Newton Police Department. I've got the number in my desk."

"That's okay," I said, "I can get it. Look, relax. He's dealing mostly with small-time punks, especially up there. The only real danger he's in is from getting kicked in the shins."

"Not lately," she said, shaking her head emphatically. "He was involved in that big bust here on the guy with the mob connections in Kansas City. I was glad they pulled him off of that when they couldn't locate the drugs. Did you hear about that deal?"

"Uh-huh," I nodded, making an effort to look uninformed. I have been told that I look that way without trying. "I thought that guy was still in custody though."

"He is, until they find the stuff, Mike says. They offered to let him plea bargain and walk away from it if he'd give them the location, but he turned them down. I guess he figures that whatever he's got out there is worth going to jail for." Her tension had dissipated, and I could see the familiar twinkle in her dark eyes.

"I guess so," I said. I was trying to figure out a way to get her to expand on Mike's involvement with the drug bust without triggering any of the alarms that he may have set when telling her about the situation. "They finally tied him in to the mob, huh?"

"I guess they think he's been supplying one of the big-shots up there," she said, leaning closer to me and lowering her voice. "They want to try to set up a positive line to this guy, and they think they could do that if they could lay their hands on the drugs. I guess this Kansas City guy is really connected. Mike said he was a big fish."

"It's not that one guy, the one they indicted on the counterfeiting charges a couple of years ago, oh hell, what was his name?"

"I don't think Mike ever said a name."

"What makes them think finding the drugs could tie them into this guy?" I asked. "I mean, surely the stuff's not sitting around in crates marked 'deliver directly to Mr. X,' for crissakes."

"I don't know," she said, shaking her head and thinking for a second. "I don't know." She bit the back of a finger and gazed at the floor behind me.

"Listen, I've gotta run. You quit worrying about Ahearn, he's too ugly for anyone to hurt. Thanks, Marcia."

"You're a real sweetheart," she said, grinning at me. "By the way, what did you want him for?"

"No big deal, he'll probably tell you."

"Oh, so you're going to be that way about it. I should have known, you two are just alike. See you, Case." She reached over and gave my arm a little squeeze and smiled up at me. It made me feel rotten about pumping her for information the way I had.

Just the same, I'd gotten a lot more out of this visit than I had hoped for. Mike might be able to help some since he'd been in on the bust. The truth of the matter was that Marcia had probably given me more information than Mike would.

I left the hospital and went by my house. The wind had blown a drift of dry brown leaves into the corner of the front porch, along the bottom edge of the storm door. I had to kick them out of the way before I could get the door open, and the leaves crackled and swirled around my feet in protest of the imposition. Once inside, I put a call in to the Newton P.D. and left word with Sergeant Collins to have Mike get a hold of me, regardless of the hour. I switched on my answering machine and headed out again. I'd decided to go see Nikki.

Nikki Belhaus had been a court-appointment about three years ago on a serious marijuana possession charge. As it turned out, she had been lucky not to have been caught up in a dealing charge, and on more than just grass. She was an enterprising young woman, and had been supplying a steady stream of all kinds of drugs to the local university community at Wichita State. WSU is an urban college with probably more than its share of drug traffic due to the makeup of the student population. Most of the students have jobs and connections elsewhere in the community and attend college on a part-time or evening basis. This means that they have a widespread network of acquaintances and, usually, plenty of money. In short, it's a dealer's gold mine and Nikki had been more than happy to do the excavating.

Her biggest problem was that she was a user right along with most of her customers. The profit margin in the drug business falls off sharply when you've got to keep yourself supplied in addition to your clientele. And the temptation to "dip in" is always so close and so real. Nikki was in pretty bad shape by the time she was busted and got me appointed to defend her. I got her off of the possession charge with probation and mandatory entrance into a drug rehabilitation program. Since I was so impressed with the miraculous results that the state-run program had achieved in the past with other users, and because I felt that I hadn't earned all of my fifty dollar maximum fee from the state, I did some personal follow up with Nikki and got her into a real-life drug rehab program with some help from Janette. Nikki's smarts and ambition got her through the program, clean, off probation and into a little antique store business of her own. She probably didn't make the kind of money selling antiques that she had dealing drugs, but the inventory didn't mysteriously disappear on her. You can't snort an eighteenth century oak chest-of-drawers up your nose.

Nikki's shop was on South Broadway in an old ramshackle house where she also lived. I hadn't seen her in a while, and I stood staring in the front windows at her for a few seconds before going in. Looking at her had always made feel sad, sorry and excited, all at the same time. She wore a dark sweater under an oversized black-and-green paisley print flannel shirt, open at the front and untucked, the sleeves rolled up above her elbows. The dark sleeves of the sweater protruded loosely down over her arms, covering her wrists, and were turned up once or twice to keep them from falling all the way down over her hands. Her lower body was behind the counter, but I could have told you from experience that she had on faded jeans and a well-worn pair of Wallabees.

It's amazing what just a few years of hard living can do to someone. It is obvious from looking at Nikki that she was once a very pretty girl. She now looks at least ten years beyond her age, has prematurely gray hair and always looks too thin, even when she is over an attractive weight for her build. Her eyes, however, remain forever youthful and undaunted. They peer green-gold from beneath the tangle of salt-and-pepper bangs right through to your soul; the piercing, all-seeing eyes of a five-year-old. Maybe her eyes were what made me go that extra mile for Nikki. Maybe I saw something there worth working to save. Or maybe I just liked her eyes for their own sake. Some guys are leg-men, others are boob-men, still others respect a shapely behind. I'm an eye man. There are, and have been, eyes that could make me do incredible, uncharacteristic things. Don't get me wrong. I enjoy all those other parts, too, but I'm a sucker for nice eyes.

Even though I was sure that Nikki stayed reasonably clean, I knew most of her friends didn't and that she would still have a pretty good ear to the ground on the local drug scene. The Matasseren bust and the subsequent search for the stash had been a big enough deal to have made the scuttlebutt circuit among the druggies. Nikki might be able to tell me at least one or two things that I didn't already know.

A cowbell jangled unhappily as I opened the door. "Well, if it's not Perry Mason," she said, looking up from a worn notebook with pages full of penciled numbers. "Hey, I thought about you yesterday. Look what came in." She leaned back behind the counter and dragged out an old balance scale

once used to weigh gold or silver. "How would this look in
your office?"

"I suppose that it symbolizes the balance of Justice," I said.
"There's no place for that in my office. The last time I dis-
pensed any justice there was when I threw a chair at some
guy who'd been beating up on his nine-year-old kid, and
come to think of it, I missed him with that chair, so you can't
even count that as true justice." I rolled my eyes and inhaled
deeply. The shop had the pleasant aroma of old wood and
leather, with just a touch of dirt and mildew thrown into the
mix, which made me feel pensive and a little bit nostalgic.

"What makes you so cynical, Case? Hell, I know you just
can't afford the damn thing."

"Not at the prices you charge in here," I said. We both
laughed. "Seriously, Nik, I need some help and information. I
think you might be able to offer both."

I told her the whole thing, from the first phone call right
through to the tidbits of information Marcia had given me. If
there was one thing I'd been able to establish with Nikki
through her long ordeal, it was a certain level of honesty and
trust. It was the only way I'd helped her work through two
years of living hell. I couldn't hold out on her now, in any
way, not even with something that didn't involve her. That
might jeopardize our relationship.

"Yeah, I heard about it," she said after I had finished. "I
didn't know the kid was that young, though. I heard she was
older."

"That probably made for juicier speculation," I said, "but
the mother tells me she's six, and she ought to know."

"Paul Matasseren's sort of a local legend among the
Heads," she said. "He's been a steady source for a long time
without any major problems, and he's pulled off some pretty
amazing deals. Everybody knows him, or knows of him. Ru-
mor has it that the 'sporting goods' are in a warehouse up by
the stockyards. My guess is that every building in the area
gets broken into within the week. Hell, that probably started

out as a theory and second-handed its way into fact. The bottom line is that the stuff could probably be just about anywhere. Same with the girl. I don't think anybody but Paul Matasseren knows. Unless, of course, your little client is holding out on you." She grinned an evil grin and drummed her pencil rapidly against the edge of the countertop.

"I can't even rule out Dallas or Kansas City," I said. She nodded. I had taken off my jacket and was creaking back and forth in an old cane-bottom rocker.

"If you want my guess," she said, "the stuff's not anywhere around here. There's too much loose talk, too much speculation. If the stuff was around, it would have been found by now." She stuck the eraser end of the pencil in her mouth and chewed on it for three or four seconds. I let her think. "Of course, I suppose it could have been found already. I know anybody who found it would keep their mouth shut and get the hell outta' Dodge. A person could get themselves killed over this one. You know, that would explain why all the talk and no action. Who knows?"

I hoped she was wrong. If the stash of drugs had been found by some disinterested party, it eliminated one of my options. As things stood, I could look for the kid, the drugs or both. No matter which I found first, it would accomplish my goal. Finding the girl only meant that I had to kidnap her back. No problem, just break out the tights and cape. If I could locate the drugs I would have a bargaining chip with which to negotiate. It ought to be a piece of cake, dealing with these hardcore, big-time, mob related, murderous bastards that steal children. Granted, my options were not too attractive to begin with, but I still didn't like having their number reduced by the possibility of Nikki's hypothesis being factual. I needed all the breaks I could get.

"There's something else you ought to know," Nikki said, interrupting my train of thought. She leaned forward and grabbed the arm of my chair. "The wife was supposed to have been in on the deal with him, I mean they dealt as a team.

Let's put it this way, I'd be real surprised if she didn't know where the stuff was."

The cowbell complained loudly and an elderly woman hunched through the door.

"Good afternoon," Nikki said.

"Hi, Honey," replied the woman, taking off her gloves. "I'm just browsing today, keep your seat."

"Okay, but if I can help you with anything, let me know."

"I'd better get moving," I said, smiling quickly at the woman as I rolled up out of the rocker. I put my jacket on and turned to face Nikki. "Thanks, Nik," I said as I reached back for the door handle.

"Be careful, Case," she said anxiously from behind the counter. "This guy's supposed to be a little nuts, and you never can tell who he might have been dealing with." She dropped the pencil onto the open notebook and looked at me earnestly.

"Always careful," I said, pulling my jacket down over the gun on my hip. "Always."

"Tough guy," Nikki commented sarcastically over the sound of the cowbell as I went out.

4

I microwaved a Tony's Frozen Pizza at home and washed it down with a Corona Beer while I watched the evening news on television. A bag of potato chips sat open on the coffee table in front of me, and I munched from it occasionally. You should always have a vegetable with dinner. The Channel 12 weathergirl told me that a cold front was moving through overnight and that we should get the first snow of the year over the weekend. She had nice legs, but her hair had so much hairspray on it that it looked like a plastic wig. Probably held up well in a thunderstorm. There was nothing on the newscast about the Matasseren situation. Public interest must have waned or the information had dried up. I had a few pieces of information that would bring the story back to life in a hurry, but no one was asking me. No one even knew they should be asking.

I had frittered away the balance of that afternoon checking on Linda Matasseren at Janette's and stopping by the office to take care of some loose ends. I also made a phone call to T. Michael Perkins, Esq., an attorney I knew in Kansas City. Michael had never told me what the "T" stood for, and I'd never really cared. I've always been suspicious of people who abbreviated their first names like that, it always seemed a little affected to me. But then again, he probably had good reason; a name like Thurgood or Tyrone. I would certainly never consider anything but an abbreviation for my middle name. Mostly, I was putting out feelers and contemplating my next move, but my call had a more specific purpose. I wanted Perkins, whom I had exchanged favors with over the years, to locate someone for me. I had a cousin named Perry Cabelli up there who had been in a couple of tight situations when he'd come to me for some help. I referred him to T. Michael Perkins, Esq., with the warning to Perkins that he might not want to have anything to do with him. I'd never really wanted to know for sure, but Perry's activities had always smacked of organized crime, and he had the family background to support the suspicion. I hadn't talked to him in quite awhile, but I thought he might turn out to be a good contact for this situation.

When I got back home, my phone machine informed me that Mike Ahearn would be at a bar called Rangler's up in Newton tonight, undercover. I was headed up there after my quick but nutritious dinner.

Newton is a small but active town about forty minutes north of Wichita. It is pretty much a bedroom community, and the bulk of its residents commute to Wichita for work. It has been, however, the source of two or three of the strangest cases I have ever handled. The folks up there in Newton do some interesting things. Maybe it's something in the water. They ought to have it checked. The drive from Wichita is direct and monotonous, a straight piece of interstate highway that you can almost drive while you're asleep. Many of the commuters do. I left my house at about 7:15 and climbed up the nearest access ramp onto I-135 at about 7:20. I live on the southeastern tip of Wichita, so the drive would take me almost an hour. It was a useful time to mull over the pieces of the puzzle I had collected so far. At 7:38, I was out of pieces to mull. I had a lot of work to do.

I found Rangler's with the assistance of a gas station attendant who looked like he probably spent quite a bit of time there. It was a big barn of a building painted kind of a sad green color, with lots of paved parking all around. I could hear the throb of the music from inside as soon as I got out of my car. Not a great place to quiz Mike about some fairly sensitive matters, especially since he had forewarned me that he would be undercover. Oh well, you take what you can get.

I knew that this might be my only chance to catch him for several days, and I couldn't afford to lose any time. It was one of the many things I knew that I didn't have much of. Time, information, assistance and, so far, luck.

They honest-to-God checked my ID at the door. It must have been strict policy, because Richard Nixon had been President when I reached legal drinking age. In fact, it was at that tender age, and at that particular point in history, that I formulated what would turn out to be the strongest and possibly only true political conviction of my lifetime. The Vietnam War was still grinding along, and the draft was in full swing. I had received my notice, as had most other young men in the country, when I turned eighteen, and I was all set to report to Kansas City for my physical the following week. Then some strange series of political and military happenings brought about decisions that set into motion a chain of events which eventually came down to affect li'l ol' me. Nixon called off the draft. Melvin Laird, the Secretary of Defense at the time, may have made the announcement, but the President at the helm got credit, as far as I was concerned, along with my eternal loyalty and gratitude. I became immediately, unquestioningly and forever a staunch supporter of Richard M. Nixon and whatever political philosophy he might espouse. I didn't care that such was not a very popular political position among my peers. Watergate was a trivial mistake, so what if the guy was almost impeached. Nixon, Nixon, he's our man.

Now, don't misunderstand what I am saying. I am a patriotic American and I believe that each of us has an ongoing obligation to support, participate in and give service to one's country. Maybe it's easier for me to take a coward's stand by arguing that I would have probably been 4-F due to my eyes and knees, even if the President had not intervened. But I will not try to tell you that I have ever felt one moment of guilt or disappointment over never having served in that unholy place called Vietnam. I had too many friends and family that did, and each of them had their own little version of hell to remember and live with. Some of them were still there, either mentally or physically. Maybe missing that action had allowed me to age very gracefully. I smiled winningly at the doorman as I thumbed my driver's license out of my billfold and handed it to him. He grunted and handed it back. Maybe it was just that I had maintained the innocent youthful look. Fat chance.

The interior of the club had several levels, all built around a dance floor and sound system in the middle. I wandered through the ground level and a sort of balcony area before I spotted Mike along the railing right next to the dance floor. I moved around into his line of sight so he could spot me and lead me into the situation. When I was sure he'd seen me, I turned and watched the couples on the dance floor.

"Mr. Casey," I heard Mike's voice shout over the din. "Over here." He motioned with his arm. He was sitting with a couple of college-age boys and a girl that was huddled under the outstretched arm of one of them. I worked my way over.

"Hi, Mike," I said loudly when I'd gotten to the railing. I was trying not to say too much so that he could steer me in a direction that would fit with his cover.

"Hey, guys," he said quickly, "this is my lawyer, Mr. Casey. He's the one who got me out of that bust last year. What're you doin' here, Mr. Casey?"

The "Mr. Casey" part was a little hard to take with a straight face from Mike, even if he didn't look any older than the kids he was with. He was wearing his hair in a bristly kind of long crewcut, had on a dark bulky sweater with a print shirt underneath, worn jeans, black high-topped leather tennis shoes and, for crissakes, an earring in his right earlobe. He fit right in.

"I think you know what I want, Mike. Your probation officer called me yesterday and said he hadn't heard from you in two months. That's not good. Can we go outside where we can talk about it?"

"Yeah, sure," he said casually. "Hey, you got any cards?"
He turned to the other three. "You never know when you're
gonna need a lawyer, and Mr. Casey here's the best." He
grinned slyly.

I knew what he was doing. If he could verify me on the
spot, he'd kill any speculation that I was a cop. I probably
looked like a cop. I hoped I had some cards on me. I dug
through my billfold trying to discern in the dim light between
the beige cards, which were my lawyer cards, and the white
ones, which were my private eye cards, without having to
actually take them out and read them. I decided that the
bunch on the left looked darker and pulled them out. I read
"James P. Casey, Attorney at Law" on the face of them as I
separated three out and tossed them on the table.

"There you go," I said, "I come up from Wichita all the
time."

Mike hopped over the railing and we headed across the
dance floor toward the front door. I glanced over at him a
couple of times as we worked our way to the exit. I couldn't
help thinking that the Detective Ahearn I was watching now
contrasted dramatically with the one I heard about during a
trial a year or so ago. I was representing Bill Hampers, who
was one of three defendants in a big marijuana dealing case.
Ahearn had been one of the undercovers involved in the final
bust. One of the defendants gave wide-eyed, graphic testi-
mony about the goings-on, especially Mike's part in the
drama. Something had gone haywire and all hell broke loose,
but one undercover cop kept his head and did what needed
to be done. Ahearn's fast thinking and deft skills kept the bad
situation from getting worse, and prevented the scene from
deteriorating into a cop massacre. As it turned out, two officers were wounded, one was dead and one of the four suspects was killed, but the death toll could have been much
higher, and the suspects could have escaped, if Mike hadn't
gone headlong into the line of fire, killed a man out of necessity and subdued the other three. By the time everyone else

caught up with him, he had the situation under control. You could tell that even the memory of the event still scared the living daylights out of the suspect giving the recount of the events. It was hard to believe that this was the same Detective Ahearn, this rough-cut little new-waver bopping his way through the crowd. All he needed was a set of headphones plugged into a Walkman on his belt and he would look completely harmless. Maybe I would suggest that he add that little detail to his cover.

In addition to having a true baby-face, Mike had the perfect build to pass as someone younger than his actual age. In high school, he had been the quintessential halfback; small but solid, lean and wiry, but compact and powerful. And fast. Very fast. In fact, one of the fastest white guys I'd ever known. In our heyday, we had made quite a combination. Our old coach was a dyed-in-the-wool purist. As the wishbone and other such new-fangled formations were all the rage, Coach Shafer stuck to the traditional "T" formation. I filled the fullback spot, with Ahearn at the right half. The left halfback spot was occupied by a black kid named Witherspoon, until somebody broke his arm in practice and he quit the team. His replacement was another black guy, bigger and slower than Witherspoon, but with a good nose for blocking. He provided the interference and Ahearn and I ran in tandem, me for power up the middle, and Mike for the outside or off-tackle breaking plays. The trio, held together by a quarterback with only an average arm but very good hands and a good head on his shoulders, did well enough to win the state championship two years in a row. Then I got hurt and quit, the quarterback moved to Cheyenne, Wyoming and Ahearn sort of lost interest. He kept playing, but his heart wasn't in it. He never quite lived up to his full potential. These days, personal discipline kept him in shape, and he still had the hard, compact body of the high school halfback. No one would guess him to be a day over twenty-three.

"So what's up, Case?" Mike asked as we walked across the parking lot.

"Cops and robbers," I said, "and I'm in the middle."

"Aren't you always?" Mike said as he waited for me to unlock my car.

"You know," he said quietly as he leaned across the top of the car, "I believe we pulled that off very nicely inside, but your car may blow the whole thing. A lawyer should drive a nicer car than this."

"Come on, Ahearn," I said in mock despair, "this is a 1976 Chevrolet Caprice four-door sedan. It's a classic American passenger automobile. They don't make them like this anymore."

"Thank God," he said, laughing. "It's ten fucking years old. Jesus Christ, the car I drive undercover is newer than this!"

"Yeah, but you're a hot-shot college kid drug dealer, you can afford better." We both chuckled.

I must confess that I am not a car enthusiast. They are not situated high on my list of priorities. A vehicle with ample room, adequate engine and the ability to start and run at my beckoning satisfies all of my basic needs and desires. The Chevy had done well for the last three years. I did go through a brief phase of auto-infatuation about two years out of law school. I owned a Porsche 912, a classic, when I was a well-paid associate with the firm of Dyer, Kellogg and Matz. It had given me great pleasure and a real feeling of success for that fourteen month period of ownership, but all of those feelings were overwhelmed by the sick, falling sensation in the pit of my stomach when I hit the inevitable pothole, backed into the unseen post or got handed the mechanic's bill. All of these events strike terror into the hearts of those who own expensive or exotic automobiles. I simply could not stand it anymore, and sold the Porsche. I no longer have those worries, headaches or mechanic's bills.

"Okay," Mike said as he climbed into my noble chariot, "what's your problem all about?"

I had to be careful of exactly what I told Mike. He was a good friend, but he was also a good cop. I knew where his priorities would lie. He saw me once or twice every other month. He had his job to do every day of every week.

I selectively told him about Linda Matasseren, the fact that her ex-husband's cohorts were putting the pressure on her to give them the location of the drugs and that she was scared and wanted my help. I had no choice but to leave out the minor detail of the kidnapping.

"Why do I always feel like there's something you're not telling me?" Mike asked when I was finished.

"Because there usually is."

"Uh-huh," he said, nodding, "there usually is. Okay, I can tell you this much: the department is convinced that Matasseren is not going to give them the drugs. He's got too much invested to give it all up for what amounts to a minor inconvenience for him. The guy's done his share of time but he's got a good shot at coming away from this without much of a sentence. I think he's willing to let things lie until it's over. He's obviously got a location he doesn't have to worry much about or a contact person who can move the merchandise. From what you're telling me, it doesn't sound like he's entrusting that job to his partners. We're not sure how long we can hold him. We may try to spring him and tail him to the stuff, but I think he's too smart to give us that kind of break. He's a pretty smooth operator."

"What about the wife?" I asked. "Do you think she's in on things?"

"I don't know," he said. "Hell, she's your client, what do you think?"

I said that I hadn't decided yet, which was true. Of course, I knew what he didn't, that her child's life was being threatened over all of this. It made me reasonably certain that she knew nothing.

As I contemplated how to urge some more information out of Ahearn without tipping my hand, I heard a sharp explosion behind my left ear, felt a sudden barrage of prickly stings on the left side of my face and sensed hundreds of tiny dull thuds against my hair and jacket. Within a fraction of a second, there was a white flash behind my eyes, inside my head, and everything went blank for an instant. At almost the same moment the left side of my skull began to send out pulsing pain signals. I wound up with my head in Mike's lap and the warm ooze of blood on my face. Mike was grabbing for his pantleg to pull his gun from an ankle holster, but I was in his way. I was already dragging my gun out from beneath my jacket. Someone had smashed in the window of the car and was now reaching through the space left vacant by the shattered glass and grappling with me for my gun. He had both arms and most of his torso inside the car and was flailing at my face with one hand while grabbing at my right arm with the other. My unrestricted left hand grasped at the door handle, unlatching the door. At the same time, my left foot came up from the floorboard, planted itself directly below my hand on the door and pushed. The torso swung immediately away from me and the voice that belonged to it cried out in pain as its lower half banged against the truck parked next to me. I kicked the door hard again and the voice grunted as I raised my gun up and leveled it at the face not three inches from the end of the barrel. My foot maintained steady pressure on the door and the man's hands went up high between the door and the car, his elbows out on either side. His lower back was wedged tightly against the big side view mirror bracket on the passenger side of the pickup truck behind him. He wasn't going anywhere.

"Don't shoot, man," he said. "Don't shoot that thing."

I heard the faint shuffle of running feet in the distance, shouts from the far side of the parking lot, car doors slam and the controlled squeal of tires as a car sped away.

I kept pressure on the door with my foot and then my shoulder as I got out of the car. The barrel of my gun stayed right on the end of the big man's nose. He was big enough that he could almost look me in the eye even though he was bent over and leaning through the door frame. Ahearn had already gotten out of the car on the other side and was running around the front to come up behind our large intruder. Mike had never reached his gun and, seeing that I had the situation under control, had wisely left it in its holster along the inside of his left calf. He looped his arm around the guy's throat and up over the door frame, putting sort of a hammer-lock on his neck, using the chrome windowcasing as a fulcrum.

"Got him," Mike said, nodding at me from behind the guy. I slowly let pressure off of the door and stepped back, putting my gun away. I instinctively raised my left coatsleeve to wipe the stickiness from the side of my face and then jerked it back. What he hell, the coat was ruined anyway. I went ahead and wiped.

I heard the shuffle of running footsteps on the concrete again, this time from the direction of the building. I looked up and saw a bouncer-type and two other guys with "Rangler's" printed above the breast pockets of their shirts running toward us. I was glad I'd gotten my gun put away. No sense making it more of a scene than it already was.

"We called the cops," the bouncer said breathlessly as they got closer. "Steve saw that guy bust out the window. We try to keep an eye on the lot. We didn't know there was anybody in the car. What the hell's goin' on?"

"This asshole must have been after my tape deck," I said, "but he didn't check to see if there was anyone in the car before he busted the window. That about right, dumbshit?"

"Fuck you," came the guttural response, strained by the pressure from Ahearn's hard arm. Famous last words.

"Jesus," said the bouncer between heavy breaths, looking at my face. "The glass do that?" He turned quickly back over his shoulder. "Larry, run back in and get this guy a towel." Larry took off at a trot.

The rest of the evening was a mess. The major results were that we were able to get the would-be thief down to the Newton Police Station without blowing Mike's cover, the station medic determined that the bump on the side of my head would be sore, but represented no serious damage and that all of the cuts on my face were superficial enough not to need further medical attention. My car was driven down to the police lot by a Harvey County Sheriff's officer. The guy had used a crowbar on the window and my head, which they found under the car. Mike was able to take an officer aside at the scene and explain his situation, so he was taken in like a witness and then allowed to monitor the questioning of the window-smasher from another room. The Newton police were very cooperative and allowed me to participate in the questioning. I had a feeling Mike had something to do with that.

A red-faced detective named Turner questioned the assailant, whose name turned out to be Arnold Moore, while a uniformed officer sat at the other end of the table and took notes. Detective Turner was about fifty, looked like an ex-military type and didn't act pleased to be where he was. He had a folded face that seemed to be attached to his skull somewhere around his eyes, and it hung heavily and loosely from the suspension points. He looked a little like those pictures you see of jet pilots taken inside the cockpit when they're pulling six or seven G's. He had a big meaty hand propped under his chin, pushing up on the heavy jowls with thumb and forefinger. Probably held everything in place that way.

"So you just cruise the lot looking for radios and then smash the windows, right?" Turner asked Moore. "But this time there just happens to be two guys sitting in the car?". Turner plucked a smoldering cigarette butt from the lip of a dirty black ashtray on the table in front of him. The butt was burned down to the point of singeing the front end of the filter. Turner held it between thumb and forefinger, turned it sideways to absently inspect the smoking ash, and poked it gingerly between his lips. He inhaled powerfully, the folds in his face moving upward to all but obliterate his eyes and the ash on the end of the cigarette glowed brightly. Turner's face was frozen in a sour expression as he held the smoke in his lungs and throat with the back of his tongue and he squashed the life out of the fiery ember with three or four deft motions in the bottom of the ashtray. His eyes watered slightly as he looked to Moore for an answer.

"It's like I told you," Moore said in exasperation, "we scoped out the car and then came back to it later. Those guys must have gotten in the car in between."

"So you were hitting several cars in one sweep," I said, "Is that right?"

"Yeah, you got it, we check 'em all out and then go back and hit 'em."

"So," I said, leaning toward Moore, "How come there weren't any other broken windows?"

He fidgeted slightly, but made a quick recovery. I'd caught him off guard, but he covered it well enough that I didn't think Turner even noticed, but then I wasn't sure that Turner would have noticed if a freight train had come rumbling through the interrogation room.

"Yours was the first one," Moore said, looking right at me. He was an impressive specimen, about six-five and large all over. He looked to be about two hundred and sixty pounds, but could have easily been more if there was as much hard muscle under the fat as it looked like there could be. He had certainly made smashing in my window and knocking me halfway out the other side of the car in one swipe look easy. He had a face that had been beaten on a few times and arms that looked like massive cables. He was overweight, with a huge belly but the arms, chest and legs showed clear signs of strength and a kind of utilitarian fitness. His face was ruddy and pockmarked, one eyelid drooped noticeably and his misshapen nose had a scar that ran down the length of the bridge and off the left side onto the nostril. He had thick black eyebrows and hair of similar color, texture and length growing out of his nose and ears. There were droplets of sweat rolling down his temples and on his upper lip, but Turner refused to let him take his coat off. Moore stunk almost unbearably in the small hot room, and I wished Turner would have figured out a different way to make him suffer. The hair on his head was cut very short and without style. It looked more like it had simply stopped growing at that length than as if it had been purposely cut that way. I hoped he hadn't paid much for the trim.

The rest of the questioning was more of the same. We couldn't go into a lot of the pertinent, meaty areas of inquiry without the possibility of blowing Mike Ahearn's cover, and I couldn't go off on a line of questioning that would tip Detective Turner off to the fact that I was working on a case. I didn't want or need any inquiry into that potentially sensitive subject. I could only hope that Ahearn would be as discreet. After the uniformed cop had escorted Moore away, Turner rubbed his face hard with both hands and exhaled slowly. The undersides of his coatsleeves were worn almost threadbare. In fact, the whole tired gray suit had seen better days. I could guess that he probably was proud of the fact that he'd only purchased three suits in his entire life. It showed.

"Friggin' low-lifes," he said, his hands still covering his eyes, "can't make an honest living, got to steal from those who can. For godsakes, I'd just as soon shoot 'em as arrest 'em. Scumbags. Fucked up my whole night." The commentary confirmed all my suspicions. Turner represented the worst possible mutation in an otherwise honorable profession. A cop's life is never easy, the everyday decisions and attitudes almost always have life and death implications. The tremendous responsibility can be dangerous in the hands of someone like Turner who has a twisted perception of law and order. Right or wrong. Us and them. Not that I was any big fan of Moore or his type, but someone like Turner who sees the world in clear divisions of black and white can be as impossible to deal with as someone like Moore if you, for any one of a lengthy list of reasons, might happen to come down on the wrong side of the clearly drawn, unwavering line. Turner's attitude evidenced ignorance and blind dogmatism. I detested him for both.

"At the epicenter of all humanity lies the basic struggle between good and evil," I said.

"Huh?" he said in dull-eyed response, staring out at me from between his leathery hands.

"Never mind," I said as I stepped through the doorway, closing the door behind me.

I walked out of the Newton Police Station at 1:15 A.M. still not sure whether the incident had been an attack on me, an attempt to unravel Ahearn's case or, like the man said, a badly bungled rip-off job. Ahearn had kept me out of the soup by not mentioning the purpose of my visit. I did know that Moore was a lot older and more physically qualified to do other sorts of illegal work than most car stereo thieves that I've run into. I also noted that he had conspicuously avoided mentioning the fact that I had pulled a gun on him. Maybe it didn't surprise him. Maybe he knew that I carried one. Or maybe he just figured it would be one more detail that the cops would get hung up on before he could post bail and get out of there. At any rate, he'd had enough smarts to leave something like that alone.

I spent the time during the drive home going over Linda Matasseren's story to see how it held up. Everyone I'd talked to about this thing seemed to be more than a little suspicious of the fact that she knew nothing of the drug operation, but nothing made sense, knowing what I knew, if she did. I would have no choice but to confront her with the degree of her involvement and try to gauge her reactions. During all of this analysis, I kept drifting off on a tangent which started with the little six-year-old Matasseren girl, kidnapped and scared to death, and wound it's way around to my own four-

year-old. As my subconscious interposed my Jennifer with
Sara Matasseren, I could, for those brief seconds, experience
firsthand the terrible helpless feeling of knowing your child
was in danger and not being able to do anything about it. If
the open driver's portal hadn't been supplying me with a
steady flow of 34-degree air, I would have been worried
about dozing off into a fitful nightmare behind the wheel.

By the time I got home, I had convinced myself, at least for
the time being, that Linda Matasseren could not possibly
know the location of the drugs. I went inside, picked up the
phone and dialed my ex-wife's number.

"Hello?" came a sleepy voice at the other end.

"Annie," I said softly, "it's Case."

"Oh, um, what's wrong? What time is it?"

"Nothing's wrong. I just wanted to... Look, tell Jenny
that I love her and give her a big hug from her Daddy when
she wakes up in the morning, okay? And tell her that I'll be
by to see her next week."

"Alright," she responded, a little more awake. "I'll also tell
her that her father is a crazy person. Case, are you okay?"

"Sure, I'm fine," I said. "Sorry to wake you. Goodnight."

Now I could go to sleep.

5

The pattern of tiny cuts on the side of my face made shaving impossible, which was all right with me. I abhor shaving. I have worn a mustache since my college days, but have never worn a beard for any length of time. I simply don't shave more than once or twice a week when I'm on vacation or working on "out-of-court" cases. Jay Price once told me that no one would ever take me seriously as a lawyer until I learned how to shave. I wasn't sure I cared.

I winced several times as I combed my hair. I accidently dragged the comb over the still tender lump just above my left ear once before remembering it was there. It was a good thing that the glass had absorbed most of the blow. Better the glass than my valuable head. I had also called upon some muscles during last night's scuffle that had been dormant for a while. They were now protesting the sudden call to action after the fact. Fortunately, they had answered the call when they were needed. They hadn't let me down yet.

I am built in such a way as to get at least a modicum of respect based just on my physical presence. For the last ten years or so, my weight has hovered around a reasonably well-formed one-hundred ninety pounds. At just an eyebrow under six feet, that puts me in the category of hefty, chunky, meaty or stocky, take your pick. Most of the bulk, however, is in my upper body, the chest and shoulders, which adds to the appearance of strength while minimizing the thickness that has developed around my middle. I have been told that I look as though I would be hard to move, and that I have a certain look in my eye, call it bluff or bad attitude, that makes most people reluctant to try. It's not hard to guess just by looking at me that I once ran footballs up and down a field, I was designed and built for the job. I have found, however, that there is a tendency for people to underestimate my ability to move my bulk and are surprised by my quickness. That mistake almost always gives me an edge, even over a larger opponent. As a rule, I have always preferred to talk my way out of any situation, but the appearance of being able to back it up never hurts. It has probably helped me avoid more confrontations than win them. I avoid when possible.

I try to stay in reasonably good shape, and I usually manage to play racquetball a couple of times a week. After a game or two at the YMCA, I usually lift some weights and play some half-court basketball to cool down. Such is the extent of my exercise routine and training program. It has been tested and proven as far as I'm concerned.

I went out to the garage to see how much of a beating my car had taken after pulling on a heavy sweater and a thick wool jacket. I was still feeling chilled from the cold drive home. It looked like the broken window was the only casualty. The driver's door had a new creak and a hitch as it opened, but it still closed solidly and there was no visible damage. I went back inside and called an auto glass place about three miles from my house. Then I called my insurance agent to make sure that broken glass was covered under my policy. He said that the glass was covered, but that there would be a fifty dollar deductible. With my luck it would cost forty-nine fifty to replace it. My final call was to Linda Matasseren. I gave her directions to the auto glass shop and asked her to pick me up there around 10:30. She was right on time.

I gave directions to a pancake restaurant as she drove. She asked about the broken glass and cuts on my face and I told her that they had nothing to do with her situation. I wasn't sure whether I was lying or not. We talked as we ate, but the conversation was strained. Probably not good for the digestive system. "I've got to ask this, Linda," I said after we'd covered some cursory questions. "I'm sorry to have to, but it's the only way I know how to help you. My contacts have told me that you were very much involved in Paul's operations. They all agree that you know more than you're telling me." I swallowed a bite of sausage and looked right at her. "Linda, are you holding out on me?"

She looked a little shocked. I had been pushing her memory up until then, convincing her that some little seemingly unimportant detail might be important. Now I was confronting her directly with the harsh reality that I knew she was not as sweet and innocent as she pretended to be. It took a minute or so of staring into her plate for her to gather herself together.

"I guess," she said after the silence, "that I'd better level with you. I know a name that's directly involved in this thing. Wiley."

"As in Wile E. Coyote?" I asked. I was trying desperately to soften the brittle mood I had created.

"Cute," she responded with a sarcastic smirk. She and Sara obviously watched Saturday morning cartoons together. "Yeah, spelled W-I-L-E-Y. I saw it written down once on something. I heard Paul call him that on the phone." She continued to stare down into her plate, directing her words and expressions at the half-eaten pancakes lying there.

"Anything more you can tell me about it?"

"Two things. My guess is he's in Dallas, because during this one month Paul seemed to talk to him a lot, and that month's phone bill had a bunch of long distance calls to Dallas on it. There were also lots of calls to Kansas City, but mostly Dallas that particular month.

"Any way you could get your hands on one of those phone bills?" I asked.

"Don't you think I'd have done that in the first place if I could?" she asked sharply narrowing her eyes. "Paul gets rid of all that type of stuff as soon as it's paid or whatever." She shook her head angrily left, then right, and locked her stare back down into the plate.

I waited a few seconds. "Okay, what's the second thing?"

She brought her hand up out of her lap and picked up her fork. She poked at a piece of pancake with it. "It has something to do with cars."

"What is 'it'? Wiley, the operation, the storage of the drugs, what?" I tried to keep myself from sounding angry and impatient, although I was feeling angry and impatient.

"I don't know," she said, looking up at me apologetically. "I would just hear Paul say things about auto things, and tires."

"Auto parts?" I said, trying to help her along.

"I don't know, maybe. Something Paul said or talked about with this guy just made me think of cars or fixing cars." I saw her eyes fill, and then two heavy tears rolled down her face. Her shoulders shook a little and then she looked back down into the plate, grappling with her napkin to wipe nose and eyes. She sniffled.

"Linda, I know this can't be any fun for you, but I can't even begin to help you if you're holding back information from me. You've got no reason not to tell me."

"I know," she said in a raspy voice. "I just . . . I don't know, I guess I didn't want you to know that I dealt drugs with Paul. I'm a mother, a good mother. I'm not a criminal. I just sort of got caught up in things with Paul. He makes so much money . . ." her sentence trailed off. "I guess I was afraid that if you knew about my involvement with the drugs you wouldn't help me. That wouldn't be fair to Sara, she's the one who really needs your help."

Ah-hah, poor Sara again. I'd fallen for that ploy once already. It's hard to play tough guy and lean on a teary-eyed mother in a moment of total fear and vulnerability. Fun work I do.

I pulled the napkin up off my lap and held it across the table to her. She took it. "I said I'd help you, and I will. I don't pass judgement on people that easily. What you've done and who you are are two different things."

She blew her nose very daintily into the napkin and looked at me with reddened eyes. "I've got a list of names that might be useful."

They were contacts of Paul's that she had not thought of earlier, or knew very little about. She didn't have any idea whether any of the names were involved in the latest caper, of which she still claimed total ignorance, except for the Wiley connection. Oh well, any leads are good leads, at least I had something solid to work on now.

As we drove back to the glass shop parking lot, I broached the topic of finances. I told her that I would be incurring some travel expenses in the next few days, but that I would try to keep them to a minimum.

I had originally said that I didn't need an expense advance or retainer, but I thought she needed to know what kind of money she was spending. She had said she didn't mind, whatever it took to find Sara. They all say that, but few remember saying it when the bill comes.

By the time I got out of the car, she seemed to have relaxed some and I leaned in the open door and asked whether or not she felt safe at Janette's. She said that she did, thanked me for the place to stay and the meal as she stepped on the gas. Standing inside the shop office watching her drive away, I could almost hear her thinking, "get off my back and get on with it." I have such an outstanding rapport with my clients. The new window was $106, so I would get at least a little piece of my premium back from the insurance company, if you cared to look at it that way. Onward, steed.

By 3:00, I was one-third of the way to Dallas. I had called an old college buddy of mine down there before I left and made arrangements to stay with him. He had a nice middle-class house in the suburbs with two unused bedrooms, and I knew it wouldn't be an imposition.

Greg Marcus and I were in the Administration of Criminal Justice program together as undergraduates at WSU. While we earned extra money moonlighting as security guards, we dreamed big dreams together of becoming hot-shot cops and eventually top police brass with some big-city force on the east coast. Greg lost interest sometime during our junior year and I came to find out that my knees and eyes weren't up to police standards. Greg wound up with a degree in business and went to work for a bank in Tulsa, Oklahoma, while I went on to law school. We'd kept in touch, and usually saw each other once or twice a year. He eventually drifted further south, winding up in Dallas, and was working for a bank down there now.

I pulled into Dallas, Mesquite to be more correct, about 6:30 that evening, stopped for a twelve-pack of beer and wound my way through the well-kept lawns to Greg's house. He greeted me in the garage with a good solid handshake and a stinging slap on the back. Greg and I always have seen about eye-to-eye, but I maintained a consistent twenty pounds over him, even as we both began to get the "heavies" through our middle and late twenties. Greg is one of those guys who have an inert sense of power about them, projecting an illusion of more size and strength than they actually possess. He always made me feel slightly smaller and lighter than him, when in fact the opposite was true. He was in much better shape than I. He had on white gym trunks and one of those T-shirts cut off just below the chest to expose the lower abdomen. There are those who will try to tell you that the purpose is to increase ventilation, but I say they're just showing off. There were wisps of sandy brown hair encircling the navel of Greg's flat stomach. I was envious, but not enough so to motivate me to undertake the effort that would be required to make my stomach look like that. Not worth it. I shrugged my shoulder against the burning sensation left by Greg's hand.

"So, how was the drive, counselor?" he asked. "You about bored stiff?" The years in Oklahoma and Texas had given him a slight drawl that always amused me a little. Acquired colloquial affectation.

"Naw," I said wryly, "they made it interesting this time. There's construction from just this side of the border all the way to just north of the Fort Worth turn-off, so you've got to keep guessing which lane you're supposed to be in. Keeps you on your toes."

Greg took my nylon gym bag and the beer, leading the way inside. "How's Annie?" he asked back over his shoulder. Ann and I had dated all through college when Greg and I were spending a lot of time together, so Greg continued to think of us as a couple, even though we'd been apart for over three years.

"Fine, I guess. She's got a new job with the telephone company in the marketing department. She seems to like it. The money's good."

"How about Jenny, is she still as pretty as her mom?" He smiled. "It's a damn good thing that kid didn't get your looks, Case. Can you imagine?"

"Very funny," I said. "I always thought she did get my looks." We both laughed while we opened the beer.

Greg walked over to the kitchen cabinet where he had left my bag, lifted it about six inches above the countertop and let in drop. The gun inside made a solid thud as it hit.

"Are we working this trip?" he asked.

"See, I always said you'd make a good detective," I smiled. "Yeah, I'm working."

We finished off the beer while I told him about the situation. Greg made a call to his girlfriend, who he said worked at a posh club downtown as a maître 'd only in this case the D was for dame. It sounded like he was uninviting her over after work. I felt a little like the intruding in-law, but I tried not to let it bother me. It was easy. At 8:30, we went out for

Chinese food and were back by 10:15, slightly stuffed and slightly drunk.

"I've gotta hit the sack," Greg said once we were inside. "I had a rough week."

"Shit," I said in mock disgust, "how does a banker have a rough week?"

"Robberies," he said, grinning, and went back to his room.

I found a half-finished bag of Nacho Cheese Doritos in the cabinet and munched on them while I watched Saturday Night Live. New York City Mayor Ed Koch was the host, with musical guest Joan Jett. I remember being groggily amused at the thought of those two getting married. I fell asleep on the couch.

6

I awoke the next morning to the smell of bacon and coffee and the rattle of dishes from the kitchen.

"There's toast, scrambled eggs and bacon in five minutes," Greg said, looking at me across the counter that divided the large kitchen from the dining room. "You know, even though you don't pay any rent and you're a generally lousy house guest, I'd still allow you to sleep in a bed."

"Oh, thanks. That's nice to know," I said, sitting up, "after you've tortured me for one night on your killer couch." I stretched my arms and rubbed my neck. I looked around the kitchen and living room, but saw no signs of anyone but Greg.

"So where's this girlfriend you speak so fondly of?" I asked. "I'm not scaring her away am I?"

"Oh, Amy?" Greg said, looking up from his skillet. "She'll be around. She sleeps in most Sundays. The club doesn't close until three and she usually doesn't get off until about four. I keep telling her to get a job with normal hours."

"And she tells you that those are normal hours."

"Uh-huh."

"Sounds like just the kind of girl who'd get your number. Just perfect. Well, at least that makes me feel better. I thought maybe you were ashamed of me."

"Oh, I am," Greg said, laughing. "But that wouldn't keep me from bringing Amy around you." He flipped a forkful of bacon grease in my direction playfully.

In the bathroom mirror, I inspected the cuts on my face. They were all but invisible now, complaining only when irritated. I left them alone to heal.

55

Two eyes stared back out of the mirror at me, sore looking eyes with very green middles which were accented by red. I remember once in grade school when my class was discussing simple genetics and relating them to eye color, a little girl described my eyes as being "the same color as a frog." She was about right. Those green eyes were also nearsighted, and they were red and sore this morning because I had neglected to take my contacts out before nodding off to sleep the night before. I wear soft lenses, but that doesn't make sleeping in them anything less than painful. I tried wearing glasses for a few years, but I could never get used to them sitting on my nose and was constantly losing or breaking them. When I was nineteen, I got my first pair of hard contact lenses, stuck those little pieces of plastic in my eyes and wore them for sixteen hours the first day. From that day forward, I only kept glasses around for emergency situations, like losing a contact. When I switched to soft lenses a few years later, it made the wearing even easier. I wear them so well, in fact, that most people I know, even close friends, aren't aware that I have anything other than perfect vision in my froggy green eyes. I took my contacts out one at a time, rinsed them in bottled saline solution and stuck them back in. Relief. I splashed cold water on my face from the bathroom tap. The bathroom smelled like a scratch-and-sniff ad out of G.Q. Magazine. There was a blow dryer, a full complement of men's face creams and hair conditioners and enough Aramis cologne to bathe a horse in; luxuries and necessities of the modern American male that were wasted on me. I dried my face on what was probably a designer bath towel.

"You know anybody in the tire or auto parts business down here named Wiley?" I asked Greg as I walked into the kitchen and gratefully accepted a steaming cup of coffee. I was considering the possibility of an auto dealership or auto repair shop, but some sort of parts operation seemed like it would be a lot more conducive to the situation. One step at a time.

"Wiley? Doesn't ring any bells. Let's check the book." We poured over the thick Dallas Metro Yellow Pages Greg pulled from beneath the phone stand while we ate our breakfast.

"No Wiley under 'tires' or 'automotive supplies,'" Greg said through a mouthful of scrambled egg. "Hey, here's Lubbins, though. Lubbins Auto Supply, they're a customer at the bank. Old Man Lubbins would know anybody in Dallas who's in the auto biz." He shoved the open book across the table at me and pointed to an ad in the upper left-hand corner.

"Sounds like a place to start," I said. "Would he know your name?"

"No, but he'll know the bank. He's been there for years. He's what is known as an old and valued customer." He fished a couple of his business cards out of a drawer by the table and slid them at me.

"Ever have any reason to think he was into anything shady?" I asked.

"I'd guess against it. I think he's worked a lot of hard years in a tough business and it's paid off for him. He probably bleeds motor oil when he gets cut. His name is Jake, but they all call him 'The Old Man'."

Greg studied the ad to see if he could remember which one of the Lubbins Auto Supply stores housed the main office. He decided that it had to be the North Dallas location. The ad said that they opened at noon on Sundays. Maybe I'd be lucky enough to catch the Old Man in the office. I went ahead and got dressed, leaving early enough to get to the store well before it opened. I headed out towards the bypass Loop that rims the outer edge of the Dallas Metroplex. The electric clock in my dash said it was 10:45.

I pulled into the North Dallas Lubbins Auto Supply parking lot at 11:10 and waited in the car watching employees arrive for work until I saw them unlock the front doors. I went in and asked a guy with a name tag that said "Shorty" where I could find Mr. Lubbins.

"Jim or the Old Man?" Shorty asked, studying my face.

"The elder Mr. Lubbins," I replied.

Shorty looked at me like I was some sort of freak and directed me up a set of stairs behind the service counter in the rear of the store, saying to turn right at the top. I could see a set of offices with half-wall windows looking out over the counter and shop from the second-floor level. The executive office suite. I went on up.

Jake Lubbins sat behind an enormous metal desk that took up two-thirds of the small office. He was swiveled around in the desk chair with his back to the door, peering out the large window onto the store activity below, engaged in a mumbled conversation on the phone. I made my way through the boxes and stacks of auto magazines and parts catalogues to the lone visitor's chair in the office, against the side wall next to a shelf loaded with various pieces of cars, many of which were used or salvage. When Lubbins finished his phone conversation he spun quickly around, hung up the phone and wrote hastily and noisily on a yellow pad in front of him on the desk. When he had finished the note, torn it from the pad, folded it up and put it in his shirt pocket, he turned his chair 45-degrees to face me and said, "Can I help you?"

He had a slightly guttural foreign accent which belied his appearance. He looked like a cattle puncher. He wore a faded blue western shirt with pearl snaps that pulled tight over his thick chest, worn jeans and cowboy boots. His mostly-gray hair and mustache were thick and sloppy and his dark skin was rugged and creased. Thick gray and black hair curled out through the gaps in the front of his shirt at the chest. You expected John Wayne's ambling drawl to come forth from his hard mouth, but instead that accented voice rolled out at me again: "Come on, I've not got all day."

I had been digging in my hip pocket for one of Greg's business cards, and I held it out to him.

"I'm sorry to bother you, Mr. Lubbins, but I'm an investigator working with Mr. Marcus at the bank and was wondering if you could help me with some information."

"What kind of investigator?" he asked with a piercing stare that went right through me.

"A private investigator," I said. Silence.

He looked at Greg's card again, stuck it in his shirt pocket and said, "Sure, what can I do?"

"I need to know if you can help me locate a man named Wiley. He's supposed to be in the auto parts or tire business."

"Sure," Lubbins said, "Wileys run the Tire Warehouse. Brothers, Bret and Paul. They're over on Independence, in the warehouse development. You know, the new warehouse place with the landscaping and all. But I don't buy tires from them. They can't match the volume discount I get through Federal. They're just local. Let's see, they go by U.S.T.W., United Suppliers Tire Warehouse."

Just then a guy leaned in the door. He was a younger version of Jake Lubbins, but with dark hair and no mustache. The body was solid and leaner, but it was draped in the same garb, with the sleeves of the western shirt rolled up two turns over large, hard forearms. It had to be Jim Lubbins.

"Sorry, Pop," he said, "but we got a truck full of shit from Cal-Custom out back that I don't find no purchase orders on. I need you to come accept it or send it back. We can't verify nothin' with their office 'cause they're closed Sundays. The driver's waiting." This one had the John Wayne voice.

"Alright," said Jake, "I'll come right down." He stood and waded through the junk toward the door. "I've got no more to say on the Wileys," he said without looking at me. He went out the door and down the stairs.

"Don't worry," I said to no one in particular, "I can find my own way out."

I spent the rest of the afternoon doing research on United Suppliers Tire Warehouse and the Wiley brothers. A search through the newspaper microfilms at the Harborough Branch of the Dallas Public Library told me that the Wileys and their business had a history, at four to five year intervals, of experiencing major fires or burglaries, that the oldest brother, Paul, had been called before a grand jury to testify in a major drug-smuggling case and that they had lost their youngest brother, Steven, in a racing accident while he was driving the drag-racer that U.S.T.W. had sponsored several years ago. That was the sum total of high points of the Wiley's lives, at least as far as the newspapers were concerned.

Greg Marcus put me in touch with a Dallas attorney who had connections in the police department, and that got me access to an unofficial Sunday afternoon rundown over the phone on the Wiley's activities that had been registered with the cops. They had a pretty full dance card, with several drug busts and assault charges, but only one conviction each. Those both arose out of the same incident, and were on a minor possession charge. They had probably both gotten probation on their first time out. The record of the youngest Wiley reflected that he had left behind a history of causing disturbances, assaulting citizens and being picked up out of the gutter in a trance. He'd been linked to a bungled bank robbery attempt, but the charges had been dismissed. My guess, based on the track record, was that he had developed a drug or drinking problem during his short life. And he was the one they let drive the race car.

After I was finished establishing the fact that Ward Cleaver was probably not the Wiley boy's father, I set out to survey their operation. I figured that I could learn more about their kind of family business during non-business hours, so I killed some time at the Galleria Mall while I waited for the evening and some darkness to roll around. The Galleria has a year-round ice-skating rink smack in the middle of the mall, and I amused myself by watching a blonde who could not have been a day over seventeen in a very nice skating skirt do figure 8's and practice spins over the ice. I finished my gourmet chocolate-chip cookie and I wandered through the Abercrombie & Fitch store to marvel at the expensive nonsense that only those with truly more money than they know what to do with would ever consider buying. A polite sales girl asked me once, a little half-heartedly, if she could help me find anything. She left me alone, in fact gave me a wide berth, after I offered her the obligatory "no thanks, I'm just looking." I must not have looked like one of the affluent upwardly mobile singles, A.U.M.S. I didn't think the acronym would catch on. I gave the rest of the mall the once over and then headed out to stalk my prey.

I had a brief moment of panic when I couldn't remember which level of the parking garage I'd parked on. I am a firm believer in the theory that we will all spend our respective afterlives in a heaven or hell of our own design. For me, hell will be a vast parking garage with an infinite number of gray concrete levels that all look alike, and I will be eternally destined to search in vain for a car that I know is there, but cannot locate. My instinct on that particular day for "yellow," however, was correct, and my classic green Chevy waited quietly there between a Toyota Land Cruiser and a dirty Jaguar XJS. Nice to be alive.

The Dallas Loop, which is composed of several lengths of multi-lane freeway, the main portion being a long curving section of Interstate 635, encircles the Dallas Metro area a full 360-degrees. I have always found it helpful to think of it as the outer edge of a huge clock face, with some of the area over around nine o'clock sort of flattened out. I had started out that morning in Mesquite, which sits at about three o'clock, worked my way up to about one-thirty to find Lubbins Auto Supply, made a trip down into the face of the clock for my visit to the library, and had worked my way back up to about twelve o'clock, where the Galleria Mall sits right off of the Loop. United Suppliers Tire Warehouse was at what I estimated to be about the 5:30 position, so I headed down that direction via the Central Expressway about an hour before dusk. After spending twenty minutes trying to figure out how the warehouse development was laid out, I happened upon the right drive and found myself cruising past three loading docks marked "U.S.T.W. SHIPPING AND RE-CEIVING." On the far end of the building were some glass doors with a small showroom behind them. Stairs and a metal railing went up to the doors. I drove down to the end of the next building and parked around the corner. There were two pickup trucks and a car parked near the steps that led up to the U.S.T.W. showroom. I could feel the adrenalin being released into my system and my mouth was dry in anticipation. It appeared that I would not be the only one working at the U.S.T.W. warehouse that evening.

I squatted behind a set of concrete steps coming out of the front of the building that I was parked behind. My eyes were just below the level of the stair landing as I leaned back against the building, so that I was well concealed but I could still survey the situation with minimal effort. By simply straining my neck and going up on my toes, the top half of my head rose above the landing and I could see from the rear side corner of the U.S.T.W. building, where there was a single metal door and steps, to the front of the building where the loading docks, glass doors and vehicles were. After forty five minutes, my neck and arches ached, but I remained at my vigil.

It had been dark for what I guessed to be about ten minutes when there was finally some activity for me to observe. It is annoying, sometimes, to not be in the habit of wearing a watch, but wearing one annoys me more, so I generally choose the lesser of the two annoyances. I have a whole drawer full of watches at home that were given to me as gifts by well-meaning friends and relatives. Most of those unquestionably fine timepieces will probably be sold at a garage sale without ever having been worn. One man's folly, another man's fortune.

The clock in my head estimated it to be about 7:30 when some men began carrying boxes out of the front of the U.S.T.W. building, down the front steps and loading them into the pickup trucks. It was hard to distinguish between the forms in the dark, but I thought that I could make out three of them. They loaded diligently until both trucks were full. At one point, one of them stepped out the door at the rear of the building and dropped something into the trash dumpster next to the stairs. The lighting from the adjoining warehouse reflected off of his blond curly hair as he stood in the darkness of the doorway. He went quickly back inside.

After finishing with the loading and locking up, all three men left; one in each pickup and the curly blond in the other car, a beat up Chevy Chevette. After resting back on my haunches for a couple of minutes I emerged from my hiding place. I stood slowly and limped across the space between the two buildings, trying to work the stiffness out of my knees. I went directly to the trash bin and fished out the two boxes that Curly had deposited there. As I held them up to catch some light, I could see that I was holding two "American Trophy" footballs; genuine leather, official size, mounted in open-front cardboard display packages. I felt a tiny click in my chest. I had finally happened upon a piece of the puzzle that fit.

I heard the sound of leather-on-sand-against-concrete behind me and to my left, and had just started to turn when I detected movement up above my head. My left arm came up instinctively and the outer plane of my elbow and upper arm took the brunt of the blow from a two-by-four that had been aimed at my head. I let my momentum carry me around to my left, spinning on the ball of my left foot. My right leg swung out, increasing the velocity of my spin and I aimed my foot in a sweeping arc at about knee level. My assailant's momentum had shifted his weight forward when the blow glanced off of my arm, and most of it was on his left leg, the one closest to me.

The heel of my heavy boot caught the outside of his left knee as the lugged sole shoved his kneecap sideways. I felt the sickening crunch of taut tendon tissue snapping and bones grinding clear through the thick boot. His knee collapsed at an odd inward angle as the impact broke my spinning motion and threw me back against the trash bin. As I reached back to break my fall I realized that my entire left arm felt nothing but a burning numbness, and would not follow my brain's command to precede my tush to the pavement. I hit flat on my ass as my head banged sharply against the dumpster.

Curly lay in front of me as I wagged my head from side to side trying to clear my vision. He was on his back, one leg straight up in the air, with the other clutched tightly against his chest. He rocked back and forth on the curve of his spine, making a crunching sound as the back of his shirt rubbed sand against the concrete. His eyes were clamped shut and he muttered "sonnuvabitch" over and over with a low moaning kind of groan in between. The sound of agony.

I scrambled to my feet, careful to rely on my right arm for support. As I raised up into a running position I snatched up one of the American Trophy footballs, wedged it under my left arm, holding both arm and box in place with my right hand, and ran like hell towards my car. As I rounded the corner of the building I could still hear Curly moaning.

I'm convinced that the man who invented the automatic transmission was a man with only one arm. My left arm was swollen and throbbing, and the fact that my old Chevy was an automatic was the only thing that kept me alive as I hurled the machine out of the warehouse complex at sixty-plus miles an hour. If I would have had to do any shifting, I would have certainly wound up as part of the trash that was backed up under the surrounding loading docks.

Pain, fear and adrenalin can do strange things to space and time. The drive back to Greg's took at least three days and I went by way of Paris, France. At one point, I would swear that I turned off of the one-way that splits underneath the Rock Island trestle just north of Stapleton Airport in Denver. But instead, somehow, I wound up in Greg's driveway exactly forty-five minutes after the time that had shown on my clock when I started the car back behind the warehouse.

Fortunately, the garage door was open and the door to the kitchen unlocked. As I stumbled in, I started to feel the clamminess of nausea come over me. I had but one desire; to make it to the bathroom. I noticed a headfull of long blond hair on the couch next to Greg as I passed the living room, but didn't respond to the greeting offered as I hurried by. I heard Greg call my name as I lurched silently down the hallway.

When Greg came into the bathroom to check on me, I was laying on my back on the floor next to the tub with a sweet-corn acid aftertaste in my mouth. Small consolation that Curly was in as bad a condition as I.

"Hey, amigo," Greg said, "too much hot sauce or too much firewater?"

"Too much two-by-four," I said, pulling my unbuttoned shirt carefully off of my shoulder and down my arm to expose the angry purple-red flesh just above my elbow that was starting to swell and bruise very rapidly. The ugly misshapen mass that had once been my arm convinced me that it would not go away by morning.

Grey inhaled sharply at the sight. "Holy shit," he said quietly. He leaned out the doorway and shouted down the hall, "Amy, I think you'd better bring us some ice."

"I think you'd better get me to a hospital," I said through clenched teeth.

Greg and Amy, who was the lovely young lady attached to the blond hair that I had glimpsed over the back of the couch, helped me out to the car, into the hospital and then back into a spare bedroom at Greg's upon our return several hours later. It was a little past 2:30 A.M. and I was of rotten disposition. The pain killer they had given me in the emergency room made me groggy, and the three-hour wait to have some resident inflict excruciating pain on me while setting the broken bone had made me cranky, to say the least. Nice to meet you, Amy.

The X-rays had shown it to be a relatively clean break of the humerus just above the elbow. They rigged me up with one of those ninety-degree angle casts that runs from hand to shoulder, anchored down by an uncomfortable blue cloth sling with velcro straps that were cinched up tightly so as to render my entire left side immobile. I had at least managed to convince them to stop the cast just above my thumb, leaving my fingers free so that I could still grasp things with the hand. Concessions like that are hard-fought when dealing with tired but zealous medical residents in the middle of the night. They got especially short with me when I tried to convince everyone that I had done the damage falling off of a ladder. Greg and Amy remained silent.

I must admit that I did have a moment of pleasure amid all the misery prior to going to bed when Amy helped me remove my contacts. The cast made it a little hard to maneuver them out of my eyes and into their storage cases, but I could pluck them out and fumble them into Amy's waiting palm, and she would rinse and store them. She did it with enough skill and confidence that I guessed her to also be a wearer. The process reminded me of the lab projects from my biology class in high school. Whenever I could finagle it, my lab partner had been another pretty blond, Sarah Hensley. I felt an empty reminiscence of those younger, more innocent days come wandering up from the depths of my memory between blinding flashes of pain before the drugs brought on a smoky numbness through the haze. Amy was a soft, fragrant vehicle to the past as we carefully transferred those fragile pieces of wet plastic from finger to palm, her nails digging small red grooves into my wrist as she tried to steady my trembling hand. Later, when I was alone in my bed, puerile thoughts of sixteen-year-old lab partners danced amidst the fog and white light in my head as I circled around the edge of sleep.

7

My head felt like it was in a vise when I woke up Monday morning and staggered forth in search of a huge glass of water to soothe the cotton-mouth I had acquired from the combination of the drugs and sleeping on my back. I found both the water and Greg in the kitchen, making breakfast. Amy was curled up on one end of the couch in a thick terrycloth robe, hugging a steaming cup of coffee. I smiled. She smiled. I felt self-conscious.

"I suppose you think all of Greg's college buddies are like me," I said to her. Her eyebrows lifted in response. "Well, we all did our best to keep ol' Marcus out of trouble. I personally felt it was my responsibility to set a good example."

Amy grinned and sipped her coffee. "He's just as warped as you said he was, Greg," she said toward the kitchen. "Let's keep him."

"I took off work today, Case," Greg said. "I figured that I could pass up an exciting day at the bank to hear all about your evening and make sure you stay in one piece. Tell me about this ladder you fell off of, and the ten-story building it must have been on top of."

"You know those goddamn doctors," I said, putting down my water for a fresh cup of coffee. "They get all uptight when you start telling them about guys attacking you with large pieces of lumber. I figured that resident would probably believe you could do this falling off a ladder. Maybe you could, who knows?"

"If anyone could figure a way, it would be you."

I proceeded to tell them all of the boring details, from my chat with Jake Lubbins to my short painful dance with the curly blond behind the warehouse. It helped me to sort back through the information and events, but I had an ulterior motive. I wanted to get Greg interested enough to recruit him as an assistant. I hoped to do some more poking around at United Suppliers Tire Warehouse, but I was a little conspicuous in my fresh white cast and attractive blue sling.

"It's too bad that guy intercepted the footballs," Greg chuckled, amused with himself. "It would be interesting to see if those tied in with your hidden treasure."

"Wait a minute," I said, jumping up and then wincing at the movement. "I did grab one of them. It must still be in the car."

Greg went out and came back tossing the package casually into the air.

"You threw it in the back seat," he said, "along with all that other shit." I have a small problem with trash in my car. It seems to make its way in, but never manages to find its way out. Sometimes I think I can hear it breeding back on the floor behind the front seat.

Greg fished a steak knife out of a kitchen drawer and brought it over to me along with the packaged football. Amy moved over closer to observe.

"You do the honors," Greg said, handing me the ball.

I opened the packaging as well as I could with one hand while Greg held it still. As carefully as possible, we examined each corner and layer of packaging, the angled folds of cardboard that held the ball in place and the small box on the back of the inside that housed the air-pump needle and a patch kit. No luck. I think we had suspected that the safest place to hide and transport would be inside the football itself, but thoroughness required that we examine all possibilities.

Greg carefully cut the laces of the ball and pierced the black rubber bladder that bulged through the opening in the leather. The air that hissed out around the knife blade smelled of stale chemicals, the same smell that takes on a charred quality when the air is released from your automobile tires on a hot day. But the bladder was empty except for the foul air. No bags of white powder wrapped in duct tape, bound together with brown paper and string. We both sighed in disappointment.

Greg then slipped the knife blade between the edge of the rubber bladder and the leather shell. As he pushed the bladder inward and downward, pieces of clear plastic became visible all the way around the edges of the leather seam. We fished six very flat bags of white powder from between the inner and outer skins, three on each side. These guys were cautious. They had gone to a lot of trouble and sacrificed quite a bit of possible shipping space to make sure the containers would withstand very close inspection. I noticed the MADE IN BRAZIL label stamped into the leather on the side of the ball as we removed the bags.

Each bag was made of clear plastic, with sharp flat edges that had been mechanically sealed. Each one was about four inches square and contained approximately half an ounce of what was presumably pure processed cocaine. That made about three ounces total in each football. Depending on the quality and the cut, we were probably looking at up to a pound of stepped-on product to the middle-man, who would unpack, cut, repackage, ship and deliver the white powder to a dealer, who would cut it up to a street value of around $95,000 for the same stuff, which by that time would have increased substantially in quantity without the contribution of any additional stock. A neat little package.

"Your friend with the two-by-four must have been cutting a little bit of the nose candy out of the shipment for himself," Greg said.

"More likely, he was into a little entrepreneurial acitvity," I said. "This would be a pretty stiff supply for someone to keep around the house for recreational purposes. Remember, he tossed another one just like this into that dumpster."

I glanced over at Greg. It seemed like a good time to pop the question.

"How about a trip out to the bad guy's hideout with me today? You up to a little detective work?"

"I was thinking that I'd never get invited," he said, grinning.

"Now wait just a minute," Amy interjected. "I think I've changed my mind about you, Case." She gave me a look that was hard to interpret. "Isn't it about time for you to leave?" She stood abruptly and exited to the bedroom.

"Is she mad?" I asked Greg.

"Naw," he said casually, "she's probably just upset that you didn't ask her to help out."

Since Greg didn't seem to be concerned about her, I wasn't going to be. I knew I had him hooked, and I needed his help. I recalled an incident from out of our past together. We were working as security guards on the eight-to-two shift at an entertainment complex that housed a bowling alley, ice-skating rink, go-cart track and miniature golf course. There was a group of high school kids who'd been trouble all evening and the night manager had one of us sort of trail along behind them. They were too young to be served beer, but they were getting it from somewhere, probably their cars, and the effect was showing. I was on the baby-sitting rotation when they got ready to leave. I noticed that they were acting squirrely, seven or eight of them hanging around the doorway of the bowling alley while two of them sat and played a table-top video machine. All at once, they were out the door and the machine had gone with them. All I could think of as I raced out the door behind them was what the damn thing probably cost. If they got away with it or busted it up, it was my ass and a hefty bill.

They'd heaved the machine into the back of a pickup truck, and the guy was just getting it started when I ran up and pulled my gun. Greg must have seen what was going on from the other end of the building, because he came out a side door and positioned himself about ten feet in front of the pickup, feet spread, gun held in two hands at arms length, aimed straight at the windshield of the truck.

There were a few very tense moments as I tried to convince the driver that it would be in his best interest to turn off the engine and have his friends carry the machine back inside. He was taking a lot of heat from his buddies in the back of the truck, all seated along the sides of the bed.

"They're just private security, toy cops," one of them shouted to him. "Hit the gas, they'll never shoot."

There was a moment of indecision in the driver's eyes, and I knew it had to go one way or the other in the next second or two.

Suddenly, out of the corner of my eye, I saw Greg's gun flash, heard the sharp bark in the night air and saw the windshield of the truck shatter into a million pieces. The passengers in the back scattered, some of them going down flat in the bed and others bouncing out onto the pavement. The driver and the passenger in the cab were on the floorboards.

"The next one goes right into the engine block," Greg said. He hadn't changed his position one inch. One of the two guys on the floor of the cab reached up and turned the ignition off. We got the video machine back inside, and the manager told the group that he wouldn't press charges, but that he didn't ever want to see any of them around there again. I'm not sure how he'd ever know. I really think he was mostly worried about the potential liability of having one of his security guards firing a pot shot at them while they sat in their truck. It didn't seem to bother Greg.

"Hey," he told the manager and I after it was all over, "I had a clear shot lined up. I didn't come within two feet of anyone in that truck, and there was nothing but concrete wall and trash behind them. In another second, I could have been a hood ornament on that punk's grill. I wasn't about to let that happen." That was it for him, issue and incident over.

The son-of-a-bitch was cocky. Underneath the calm banker's facade, I knew that he still was.

It took about an hour for us to come up a with a plan and do the appropriate outfitting. Greg, the sentimental sap, had kept our old security guard uniforms from the last job we'd worked together. With a little bit of replacement, removal and adjustment of trim and markings, and no adjustment of the waist on the pants, amn him, one of the uniforms closely resembled Greg's best recollection of a Dallas County Fire Inspector's uniform. Armed with a clipboard and flashlight, Greg was confident that he could sell the role. I thought he needed a hat.

We took his car, in case mine might look familiar to anyone who'd been around the night before, and headed out to United Suppliers Tire Warehouse. We had worked out a system whereby I could keep tabs on Greg's well-being while he was inside the warehouse without risking my being seen by Curly, if he happened to be around. As we pulled into the parking area opposite U.S.T.W., Greg loaded a sizable wad of chewing tobacco, purchased at a grocery store on our way, into his cheek. I hoped it wouldn't make him sick. We had agreed that if he didn't appear on the front loading area at least every fifteen minutes to casually spatter brown juice on the parking lot rather than inside the building, I was to assume that he was having difficulty or otherwise being detained against his will. I waited in the car, slumped so that I could observe without being too noticeable, while Greg sauntered in to begin his fire inspection.

His getup looked authentic enough, if you didn't know precisely what a Dallas County Fire Inspector was supposed to look like, and the clipboard loaded with "Fire Inspection Report" forms that we had dummied up from some bank documents added a nice touch. I still thought that we should have fixed him up with an appropriate-looking hat, but it seemed to bother me more than it did Greg, and he was the one going in, not I. He had the right look. Clean-cut, confident in the authority that the uniform gave him, self-conscious of the power he held on the clipboard; the ability to close a business down, at his discretion, no questions asked. His attitude was right in line with the fire inspector types that I'd dealt with in the past, pompous bureaucrats with an unending thirst for respect, no matter how achieved. I realized that he came by the swaggering arrogance naturally. Like I said, he was cocky. He had to keep it stuffed tightly down inside his banker's pin-stripe most of the time, but in this odd set of circumstances he could let it all hang out. It made me feel more secure about pulling off our plan.

The plan for our search of the U.S.T.W. warehouse was that Greg would announce to the person in charge that they were due for their routine fire inspection and that he would have to look around the premises. We hoped that this ploy would allow him to poke around at will without arousing any suspicions. We'd worked out a couple of emergency scenarios in case the U.S.T.W. people wanted to verify his identification or check with the fire department. To the best of Greg's recollection, the fire department did not normally phone ahead and schedule routine inspections, at least not at the bank. I hoped he was right.

Greg was inside for over half an hour, stepping out onto the loading platform three times to relieve himself of the tobacco juice. When he was finally finished, he walked out of the front U.S.T.W. doors and directly over the adjoining warehouse area marked only by a large yellow sign with BENNY'S painted across it. We had discussed this move. It meant that he felt some suspicion over his visit or some awareness of my presence out front, and rather than walk right out and climb into a civilian car with me waiting inside, he would continue on to the next place of business as if he were simply doing several warehouse inspections at one time. I was to drive around to the end of the building, out of sight from the U.S.T.W. frontage, and wait for him there. I waited for a nervous twenty minutes before he showed up.

"Sorry it took so long," Greg said as he got in the car, "I had to do a halfway believable job in that second place, in case they check up on me. Nervous bunch of clowns at that U.S.T.W. place."

"Okay, already, so they're nervous. What'd you find?"

"I went through every area, accounting for all the floor space in their layout and didn't see anything that would indicate that they were running a drug operation or that they were holding a kidnap victim anywhere inside. The drugs are easy to hide, but I can tell you that there's nowhere in there they could have that little girl hidden. Most of what's in there is tires on big racks in wide open areas, with a couple small offices that they let me into. I'm certain the girl's not there."

A dead end as far as little Sara was concerned, but I could now tie U.S.T.W. in with a drug operation that smelled very much like the one Paul Matasseren was involved in. At least it hadn't been a wasted trip.

Back at Greg's, I insisted on packing my belongings into my bag myself with my one good hand. Just as I was ready to depart, Amy appeared in jeans and a loose T-shirt, her long hair wrapped up on top of her head in a green towel. She sent me on my way with a squeeze around the waist and a tin full of caramel popcorn. I told Greg that I might end up coming back to follow up on the Wileys, but that I had some other things I needed to check out before I chewed on that bone any more.

It was about two in the afternoon and raining outside when I thanked him for the generous hospitality and pointed my car toward home. It rained on me almost the entire six-hour drive, and I had a strange comic book vision in my head of this black cloud no larger than my car hovering directly over me as I sped along, dumping a steady flow of depression and rain directly on my little corner of the world. The thought amused and angered me simultaneously. I had been feeling that way a lot lately. Last month would have been my ninth wedding anniversary, if Annie and I hadn't split up. The divorce had been finalized two years ago. That same black cloud had been following me around since the evening of the anniversary date, when I found myself watching a football game on a huge TV set in a bar with some people I had met only a couple of hours earlier. The women were cloying and unconvincingly interested in the game. I was on my fifth or sixth vodka and tonic. All at once I had this burning pain in my chest as I realized that I was lonely and sad in the midst of instantly intimate friends having what might appear to be a great deal of fun. I offended a redhead in a denim outfit and snakeskin boots when I got suddenly quiet and excused myself from the festivities, claiming an early court appearance. I went home and laid awake until the wee hours of morning while the bed spun slowly and cursed the black cloud drenching me with smothering depression. I remember trying to focus back on the times in my life when I had made questionable decisions or misjudged my priorities, trying to get a handle on where I might have started down the road that had led me to such a miserable place. I gave up when the incidents and turning points got so numerous that I began to scramble them in my head. Fun and games. Waking and dreaming. Life and death.

I was so groggy, tired and sore by the time I made it home from Dallas that I took a shower and fell into bed without checking on Linda. I hadn't talked to her in two days and it made me feel remiss in my duties, but not remiss enough to make me lift my bandaged body up off the mattress and pick up the phone.

8

The phone rang at nine A.M., waking me up. It was Greg.

"I got a most interesting phone call first thing this morning after I got to the bank," he said. "Old Man Lubbins was asking about what sort of investigation you were conducting for me, were you indeed authorized and that sort of thing. He seemed a little bothered."

"Very interesting," I mumbled into the phone. I massaged my forehead in an attempt to clear my mind. "You know the guy," I said, "what does that mean to you?"

"First of all," he said, "I don't know him well at all. I do know he's a pretty shrewd and careful kind of guy. I mean, anyone who's a successful independent businessman like him has to be."

"Uh-huh," I said. I wanted to hear more, and I was still trying to wake up.

"I got the feeling he was more than just curious," Greg went on. "He was very careful to sound casual, business as usual, about it. He didn't come off that way."

"So you think he's got some connection to the U.S.T.W. operation?"

"Not directly, he's too careful for that. If I had to take a stab in the dark, I'd say maybe the kid was involved, and the Old Man was trying to keep his ass out of the sling."

"Does the kid have any history?" I asked.

"No, not that I know of. But I'll tell you what. He's got no involvement at all in the business. As far as I know, he can't even sign on the company accounts."

"Sounds like maybe the Old Man has some reason to keep a tight reign on him."

"Or maybe he just likes to maintain total control over his company. An iron fist and all that."

"Um-hm," I said, thinking it over. "If you come across anything else or have any bright ideas, get back to me."

"You know it, Case. This is a hell of a lot more fun than running credit checks."

I thanked Greg for the information and input, trying to concentrate on it while I nestled back into my pillow.

As on more than one occasion in my work, I thought of a lesson I'd carried with me for years. It originated out of an experience from deep in my childhood, from a time when I was about ten years old and helped my grandfather clear hornet's nests out of his big old barn. He explained to me at length how to tell where the nests would be and how to locate them. Then he showed me. It was a slow and careful process, and it took us the better part of an entire day to eradicate the four nests which were in that barn, but I never forgot the process, the hunt, the precautions. And I never got stung, not once.

Taking on a project like looking for a kidnapped person or a missing person that doesn't want to be found is a lot like trying to locate a hornet's nest. You follow the first hornet you see until it heads for home. As it gets closer to its hideaway, you have to be more careful and more observant. At some point, when you're near the nest, the hornet will inevitably disappear. They are very careful to protect the location of their home base. If you're careful, and if you poke around gently, you generate little buzzes of annoyance that help you hone in on your target without tripping the major alarm that brings those nasty bastards swarming. The secret is to locate the nest and administer the killing dose of poison before that alarm goes off. Get too close without knowing it, or poke around too randomly or carelessly and you get stung. It seemed that my activities had prompted a little buzzing from the Lubbins'. It could be pure curiosity, or it could mean that I was getting close to the nest.

I liked the way the Lubbins fit into the picture. Jake himself had told me that U.S.T.W. was "just local" and that Lubbins had stores "all over." It made sense that a distribution ring this sophisticated had more behind it than just the lil' ol' Wiley boys. Jake Lubbins and son certainly fit the bill, and they were concerned by the fact that I had come around asking about their messenger boys. Perhaps they'd even heard about an intruder poking around at the warehouse right after a shipment went out. It made sense. However, I still had a lot of good information that pointed to a link with the Kansas City mob, and I couldn't make that connection yet, so that would have to be my next step. Keep poking.

As I lay there trying to recollect my impressions about Jake Lubbins from our brief meeting, it occurred to me that Greg and I had left the cocaine, still in its sporty packaging, stuffed in the back of a closet in his basement. Oh well, he was a resourceful fellow, he'd figure out a way to dispose of it. Momentary thoughts of sale and use flickered through my head. That was a lot of temptation to resist. Then I remembered that it was Greg Marcus, in his starched white shirt and banker's suit, that I was talking about. Greg, who worked out three times a week and ate health food. Mr. Marcus, who dealt with hundreds of thousands, even millions, of dollars of other people's money each week at the bank. He would probably flush the stuff away.

The phone rang again. I resigned myself to the fact that I wasn't going back to sleep.

"Case, is this you?" It was Mark Glennings.

"Yeah," I said, "what's the matter?"

"Didn't you get my messages?" He sounded slightly delirious.

"I haven't listened to them yet," I mumbled, but I don't think he heard me. He ran over the end of my mumble in a hasty, breathless voice.

"Janette's in the hospital, Case. Some guy broke in and roughed them up. I only went out for a few minutes to pick up a pizza. He busted the whole latch out of the front door and just walked right in."

I was now wide awake. I calmed him down enough to get the details.

Mark had gone to pick up a pizza, and as soon as he left someone had tried the front door and, finding it locked, had slipped a crowbar into the frame and busted the damn thing open. This person, who turned out to be a big, rough-looking guy, then proceeded to scare the hell out of Linda and Janette, going after them with the crowbar. Linda escaped with some nasty bruises on her legs and ribs, but Janette caught a blow to the side of the head after she tried to plant a lamp, shade and all, into the top of the guy's skull. The fun and games ended when Mark's car swung in the drive. Fortunately, the pizza place was right around the corner and it had been ready when Mark got there. The attacker fled through the back door, leaving Linda sore and crying and Janette bleeding and semi-conscious. The whole wretched incident had taken less than ten minutes.

I showered, dressed and made a beeline for the hospital. Janette looked pretty good for someone with a concussion. They had her head wrapped up in a lot of gauze bandaging and she said it had taken eleven stitches to close the gash, but that the concussion wasn't serious.

Janette and Linda had played things pretty close to the vest with the police. They told them that they had been watching TV with the lights off when Mark left, and that the guy must have thought that everyone was gone. They must have surprised him when he came through the door and he went a little crazy, then took off when Mark came back. It was believable, and a reasonable facsimile of the truth, but I did not feel good about putting Janette in a position where she felt compelled to lie to the police. I was sure that it was her, concussion and all, who'd had the presence of mind to fabricate a story which was right on the edge of the truth, but that would not arouse any undue suspicions which might throw a wrench into the work I was doing. Mark was oddly silent through all of the explanation, and I could tell that he had been reluctant to follow Janette's lead and was more than a little bit pissed at me. I couldn't say I blamed him.

In fact, I'd have to say that I was on his side. I was a real jerk, not only for this incident, but in general. Janette seemed to be the beneficiary of way more than her fair share of the ill will generated by my odd-lot of business and personal involvements. This hospitalization was by far the most severe to date, but in the time that she had been with me she had spent many hours directly in the line of fire; soothing the client enraged by my unavailability at a crucial moment, fighting off the violent husband hellbent on bending me into new and unexplored positions and fielding the unpredictable variety of phone calls which are aimed at me from time to time; death threats, missed dates, dissatisfied clients of all kinds, spurned lovers and hostile attorneys on the other side of a case. There are times when I swear that Janette practices more law than I do. Because of the nature of my dual professions, coupled with my preponderance to take on "special projects," I spend quite a bit of time out of the office. Many times, in fact, I'm not in the office for weeks on end, taking the paperwork home or on the road with me. Janette, however, is always there, a sitting duck for any asshole or crazy that might want to take pot shots of one kind or another at me. This time I had put her too close to the fire, directly in the path of physical danger. For that exposure, and for this result, I felt like a jerk, and guilty as hell.

I shuffled and paced around with my hands in my pockets while she tried to convince me that it was okay, that she knew all the risks of being in the same hemisphere with me. It seemed to me that I imposed those same risks on a lot of people. Too many.

I laid a kiss on Janette's forehead and swore to her that I'd never put her in that kind of jam again. That is, if she'd still work for me. As I straightened up from her bed, I forgot that

I had removed the uncomfortable sling from my cast and it accidently swung heavily into her side. She winced in pain as the plaster impacted an area that had been bruised by the crowbar.

"Sorry," I said, fuming at myself. A fine pair we were. We could get a flag, a fife and a drum and march down main street on the Fourth of July.

As I turned to go, I took another look at her. She looked very small and frail in the big hospital bed, with the funny, cock-eyed turban bandage looking almost comical on her petite head. A gutsy, very pretty lady. I glanced at Mark uneasily and with more than a little bit of envy as I left the hospital room.

I practically ran down the corridors of the hospital on my way out. The only thing more agonizing than facing Janette had been spending the obligatory time up there in her room, where I could do nothing whatsoever about tracking down the assailant and tying him in to the overall scheme of things. It was pretty clear to me that he fit in somehow.

Mark had taken Linda to his apartment after getting Janette admitted to the hospital. I headed over there with a feeling of dread that grew as I got closer. Janette had made some comments about the attack that led me to believe that I might know who had done it, but I hadn't wanted to question her. I had no choice but to question Linda. I was also discouraged by the prospect of having to relocate Linda. If they'd found her once, they could find her again.

I saw the peek-hole on Mark's apartment door darken as I heard Linda's voice come through the wood.

"That you, Mr. Casey?" she asked. I could hear the strain in her voice, even though it was muffled by the thick door.

"Uh-huh," I mumbled absently. There was a short silence, and then I realized that the lighting in the hallway was very dim and that she probably couldn't see me through the viewer. "Oh, yeah, Linda, it's me, Case." I mentally kicked myself for that first half-ass salutation. But then again, it was a good test. I'd have really laid into her if she'd have opened up to no more than that.

She opened the door, unlatching the deadbolt, key-lock and chain. Good girl.

Once inside, I was treated to more of the handiwork of the attacker. Linda's posture leaned heavily to the left, and the limp with each step was accompanied by a series of painful grimaces. There were visible bruises on her arm and neck, and probably more where I couldn't see them. I kept telling myself how lucky it was that neither of them had been hurt more seriously than they were. I wondered if that had been the intent. Beneath the disheveled exterior, I sensed the anxiety of a fretful she-lion worried for her missing cub. The concern evidenced itself in subtle physical signs; deep lines around her mouth and eyes, chewed and broken fingernails and a heavy pressure that seemed to give her shoulders a rounded stoop and her face a puffy softness. She didn't seem to be able to concentrate and her eyes had a dull glaze to them. I felt much the same as she looked.

I had her give me the whole, unedited version of the story; details, descriptions, impressions. From what she told me, I was able to verify my uncomfortable suspicion as to the identity of the assailant. It had been Moore, the guy from the parking lot up in Newton. He seemed to enjoy beating hell out of things with heavy hand tools. That I knew it was Moore had less to do with my deft interview skills and superb deductive reasoning, and more to do with the fact that he had been wearing the same jacket as he was the night he broke my car window, and Linda had described it in careful detail; a blue down-filled, waist length canvas coat with a "Marlboro" patch over the breast pocket. It was probably a promotional enticement or a prize from a contest, and there were probably plenty of them around, but it was distinctive enough that, draped over a frame the size of Moore's, it identified him without much question.

I took Linda to my house. I knew it wasn't a good move for purposes of concealing her, but at least I wasn't imposing on Mark. I set her up in the spare bedroom and went out to listen to my answering machine while she made herself at home. The light on the machine had been blinking as we walked in.

The lone message was from my cousin in Kansas City. Perry said that his attorney had called and asked him to call me at this number, so he was calling, and what does he get but a fucking recording. A cordial and pleasant fellow.

I dialed the number that he'd left on the machine. We arranged to meet the following morning at the Ramada Inn where I planned to stay up there.

Perry had always given me the creeps, even when we played together as kids when the family got together over the holidays. He had a cold streak of something evil in him that made him constantly do those things which made others at best uncomfortable or at worst made their stomachs turn, and he did them with a smile on his face. From blowing up live frogs with firecrackers to breaking out all of the windows in a vacant house, he had a perverse sense of adventure. Boy's games, however, oft-times turn into men's work and I shuddered to think of what kinds of things he would do for money now. I needed him, though; he was about as fast a conduit to the kind of information that I was after as I could think of, and he owed me a favor. He certainly wouldn't go running his mouth off about the kind of information he'd given out to his lawyer cousin from Wichita, or the kinds of questions that were being asked. I had him in a corner in that respect.

As I rewound the tape and switched the answering machine back on, I noticed a rubber band on the counter by the phone. I pulled the phone away from the wall, and could see that the long cord that ran from the modular jack in the wall to the phone was stuffed loosely between the back of the instrument and the back of the counter. The rubber band had popped loose from its place holding the wound-up cord together. I rarely moved the phone farther than the edge of the counter, and had gotten tired of wrestling with the tangled-up mess of the ten-foot cord that had come with the phone, so I'd secured the unused portion with the rubber band, leaving me about a foot and a half of cord to work with, and eliminating the mess. It had been that way for over a year. The only way it would have come loose would have been for someone to pull the phone beyond its shortened range, and then put it back, not realizing that the rubber band had been holding things in place. Someone had used my phone while I was gone. I went swiftly from room to room, scanning for things out of place, objects that had been moved. When you live alone, you get very accustomed to everything being in its place. After all, if it moves, you're the one who moved it. I checked my guns. Undisturbed. The evidence of intrusion was minor and generally well-concealed, but an alerted eye told me that while nothing was missing or damaged, someone had been through every room in the house, examining things inside and out. I saw no evidence of how the intruder had gained access; no broken window panes, splintered door jams or mangled locks. It had been a slick, thorough and professional job. It shook me up more than just a little. I did not want Linda to know about the intrusion or my reaction.

I shouted down the hall to her that I was going to run next door and would be right back. I was going over to see if I could catch my neighbor at home. He was a fireman, and I was hoping that he was on an off-duty rotation. He happened to be, and was busy feeding his seven-month-old son when I rang the bell. He shouted for me to come on in, it was open. He said his wife, who was an emergency trauma nurse, had been called in to the hospital. I asked him if he'd seen anyone around or in my house the last couple of days, and he said that he hadn't. He couldn't even recollect his dog barking, and it generally raises a ruckus when anyone sets foot in their yard or those of the adjoining houses. I explained, with as little detail as possible, that I was going to have to leave town and that the young woman staying in my house might possibly be in danger. I didn't want to make him think it was any worse than it was, but I also wanted to make sure he understood that it was a volatile enough situation to warrant extreme caution on his part, and bringing in the police if necessary. We had talked enough over beer and backyard barbecue that I knew he understood the nature of some of my work. I wouldn't have left him with the responsibility if I hadn't been sure of that. The request was like a gauntlet thrown down before him, with instant acceptance of the challenge showing in his eyes.

"She's taken care of," he said, and I believed him. He was a big bruiser and, although I'd never had occasion to find out, he looked like he could be mean as hell. A couple of years ago the Wichita fire department went on a fitness kick, with a goal of losing and maintaining certain weight and fitness levels for all active firefighters. The results had been rather impressive. To this day, you still see the on-duty boys jogging around the station house or working out in the side yards. You can almost spot a local fireman by his physique, the training program was that thorough and effective. I'd always thought the cops ought to do the same thing, some of our uniformed officers are an embarrassment. The department, however, evidently didn't feel that way, and no one had sought my opinion.

As I stacked clothing and supplies on my bed and packed them into my gym bag, I briefed Linda on a few rules and procedures that would be in force while I was gone. She stood in the doorway with her arms crossed, looking a little defiant. I didn't really care how defiant she was feeling, I wanted to make sure that she wasn't going to make an easy target out of herself, in case anyone was interested. I went through the locks, phones, escape routes and, finally, weapons. I showed her where my guns were hidden, and made her watch while I thumbed six cartridges into the .38. I had her hold it and pull the hammer back so it wouldn't feel foreign to her if she had to do it under pressure. I was relieved to see that she didn't have the usual clumsy discomfort with a handgun that most amateurs get caught up with. She probably sensed that her life might depend on being able to get this hunk of metal to work for her. Even though she asked a couple of patently stupid questions, she seemed to get the hang of it. I figured she would only be good for one shot, but that might be all she'd need. I wrote down phone numbers for the next door neighbors and my motel. It was all I could think of to do short of staying there with her. Kansas City was a necessity. Everything pointed there. I left with a knot in my stomach.

As I headed north on the turnpike toward Kansas City, I stewed over Moore's antics with the crowbar. He was trying to scare me or Linda, or was trying to send some sort of message to one or both of us. Either way, he was certainly acting as hired muscle for someone, someone who didn't like what one of us had been doing or what we knew about them. Linda had sworn she didn't recognize Moore and I believed her. There had been no telltale shifts in eye contact, involuntary swallowing or nervous fidgets like those that had given her away the other times I felt like she had been giving me less than the entire story. The fact that I was aware of those signs bothered me mainly because I had not yet catalogued and classified all the bits of information which they had accompanied. I wasn't sure exactly what parts of her story were incomplete or inaccurate, but I had this nagging feeling that such was the case. In other words, I was flying blind.

All the driving and activity of the last few days was beginning to wear on me. It all seemed to be happening within a very condensed pocket of space and time, but every event made me more aware of the pressing danger that the little Matasseren girl was in and made me feel as if it all were taking much too long to unwind. And to make matters even worse, I was annoying someone enough for them to let me know about it. If I slowed things down right now, I might end up with the girl's body in the front seat of my car, just to remove my reason for poking around. If I pushed too hard and too fast, I might get the same result as an act of desperation or defiance. Either way, it would be my involvement that would prompt the response. Buzz, buzz, I could hear the hornets swarming.

9

When I left Wichita, it had been no more than a dreary, drizzly day. It was now sleeting and snowing intermittently, and that forced me to keep my mind on the driving. Kansas can exhibit a nasty and unpredictable disposition from November on. The first cold snap that moves in can freeze everything in sight within an hour, and you're still habitually reaching for the air-conditioning control as you get into your car, the change from hot and humid to cold and frigid can be that rapid. They say that if you don't like the weather in Kansas, just wait a few hours and it will most surely change. That's not far from the truth.

By the time I was just north of Emporia, the conditions had so drastically changed that I was fighting to keep the car from sliding off onto the shoulder, the wipers were crusted over with ice and my toes were cold. I flipped the heat and defrost both on to high. The sound of the blower fan was almost audible above the music. I reached down and cranked a few more of the thirty-five watts per channel into the big speakers mounted in the rear deck. The Rolling Stones' "Goat's Head Soup" was in the cassette deck. Rock n' Roll, loud is the only way to listen to it. I nudged the volume right up to the edge of distortion and discomfort.

The Ramada Inn I'd opted to come back to was right off of Interstate 70 on the Missouri side of K.C. I had stayed there a couple of times en route to St. Louis. The overnight stop broke up the drive nicely. The rooms had always been spotless, the service friendly and the food in the restaurant good.

I checked in and made a collect call home. I'd shown Linda how to monitor the calls coming in on the machine so that she could pick up and answer when she heard the operator telling me that we had reached an answering device. I grinned to myself as the operator tried to place the call and was interrupted by my comforting voice, asking her to please leave a message at the sound of the beep. Just as she was telling me, in that nasal tone which all telephone operators everywhere have, that she was "sorry, sir, that number answers with a recording," Linda picked it up and said she'd accept the call.

"I'm glad you finally called," she said after the operator was off the line. I could detect a slight edge in her voice. "They called me, here, a little while ago. They left a message on the machine that said they knew I was here alone and that I'd better answer the phone the next time it rang, so I did. It was a guy who said he was in business with Paul. He said I had made a big mistake by bringing you into it and that..." she paused. I couldn't tell if she was crying, catching her breath or lighting a cigarette. "They said that I had until Friday at noon to give them the location of the shipment or Sara would be dead. I told him I didn't know where it was and he laughed." She sniffled. I could tell now that she was crying. "Jesus God, Case, I don't know where it is."

I knew that she was scared to death and had a right to be. I told her all that had changed was our time frame and then got some details from her on the conversation and the instructions they had given her for relaying the information to them. There wasn't much that sounded very useful. They had given her a Wichita phone number and a designated message to leave when she called. The probability of the number they had given her ringing a pay phone somewhere was extremely high. And once the message had been received and relayed, their call back to her could come from anywhere. It might be possible to set up the person who would take the call, but in all likelihood they would know nothing other than the fact that someone had paid them a couple hundred bucks to relay a message, to who and from who they don't even want to know. These things are so easy to set up, simple to execute and foolproof in function that it's dumb not to take the precaution. I was not so naive as to think for a minute that these people were dumb. I kept telling myself that the only difference between now and before Linda had received the call was that we had a deadline. I don't like deadlines. There's something about the word that gives them too much importance. Maybe in this instance, however, it was appropriate.

After I got her calmed down, I dialed Detective Hulmer's number at the Wichita Police Department. Detective Tom Hulmer had been the duty officer on all of my beat training and active-duty interaction during my undergraduate Administration of Criminal Justice and pre-police training days. He always used to call us "goddamned college boy police kids," and would shake his head and say that we might become policemen, but we'd never be cops. Despite his lambasting, I learned that he had a healthy respect for education. He served as duty officer for the in-service program for six years, and then became the Police/University liaison for six more. He passed the torch a couple of years ago and had gone back to a full-time detective assignment. He was a lifetime cop, damn good at what he did and damn proud of it. He'd also always harbored a little bit of sly respect for my unorthodox attitude when it came to cutting through the bullshit. When I made the decision to go to law school, he made a comment that I still remember and puzzle over from time to time. "Casey," he said, "you'd make a damn good cop. You'll make a damn good lawyer. You'd make a damn good sailor and a piss-poor marine. Good luck to ya." I'd never been completely sure whether it had been an insult or a compliment, but the slap on the back and the handshake told me that at least the "good luck" part was sincere.

Hulmer had never been particularly easy to talk to, especially over the phone. In addition, his matter-of-fact approach to life made it very difficult to be indirect or vague with him.

I tried, for several minutes, to enlist his help with only minimal explanation of my needs and the situation, to no avail.

"Cut the crap, kid," he finally said. "Tell me what the hell's going on and what it is you want, or let me go back to work." I could hear him slurping coffee next to the phone receiver.

"I've got a client," I said reluctantly, "staying at my house. She's been attacked once, and I have reason to think someone may go after her again."

"Anyone I know?" he asked.

"Linda Matasseren."

"I see," he said, trying not to sound as interested as he was. "Are you paid protection or legal counsel?"

"A little of both," I said, "but I could use your help on the protection end."

"Is this missy guilty of anything I should know about?"

"Not that I know of," I responded quickly. "I'm specifically trying to keep her out of any involvement with her husband." It was true.

"Hmmm," Hulmer buzzed over the line. I knew I wouldn't sell him. I just needed to nudge him over the line far enough to give me some support.

"These people have given her a number to contact in case she decides to cooperate," I went on. Also true.

"Then give it to me, Case. Before you waste any more of my time, is there anything else you know you need to tell me?"

I hesitated for a second. I wasn't sure whether the question was an open-ended hint that he knew more than I thought he did, or just a direct solicitation of information. "Not a thing," I said. Once again, I spoke the truth. My needs were very limited at the time.

I got him to agree to have a patrol car cruise my house occasionally without making a scene or contacting Linda. Just make sure things stay peaceful and calm in suburbia. I gave him the number that the caller had left with Linda so he could track down the location. Although I figured it was wasted time, it was the W.P.D.'s time being wasted, not mine. I'm a taxpayer, I'm entitled once in awhile. And there was always the longshot chance hovering out there.

I went down to the restaurant to have an early dinner or late lunch, it was just about halfway between the standard time for either one. I watched the snow and slush pile up on the parking lot and listened to the traffic slop along I-70 in the mush. The waitress had little to do at that time of the afternoon but take care of me, and my attention soon shifted from the cars and weather to her. She was small and dark and it took me until about her third visit to my table to realize that she had slightly oriental features. It threw me, because before I'd noticed the facial features her faint southern drawl had registered on my ears. It made for a rather unique combination.

When she came back to my table with the coffee pot, I noticed that her name tag said "Penny."

"I thought there for a while you were out of it completely," she said. "Nice to see you're still with us."

I motioned for more coffee. "Sorry," I said, "my mind was a million miles away."

Her eyes sparkled. They were nice wide almond-shaped eyes, the color of lacquered walnut. Her facial features were an attractive combination of Anglo and Asian. Narrow, slightly pointed nose and narrow forehead, but the traditional Asian wideness through the cheekbones and jaw. Small rosebud mouth, with smile lines at the corners. Hair not quite as dark or silken as most Asians and with more body.

She glanced at my cast.

"Slip and fall on the ice?" she asked mischievously.

"You might say that," I said, shifting my gaze to my steaming coffee cup. When I looked back up, her face registered understanding. She nodded and dropped the subject.

"Where are you from?" I asked.

Her eyes did a quick scan of the other tables in her area to make sure that no one wanted her attention, and then said,

"Louisiana," as she wiped a towel across the unused portion of my table while adjusting the salt and pepper shakers, napkin dispenser and the little plastic sign that displayed the daily specials. I grinned.

"I know," she said, smiling, "most people have the same reaction. I'm half Japanese, from my mother's side. She married my father while he was stationed over there in the Service. I was born in Tokyo, and we lived there for fourteen years. I went to school there, but at American Service schools. We came stateside to California for about three years, and then moved to Baton Rouge when my father retired from the Navy. My folks still live there, so that's where I say I'm from. I lived there for a little over ten years. I moved up here two years ago."

"It makes for an interesting accent," I said.

"Oh, it's mostly Louisiana," she giggled and scanned the room again. "I'll be right back."

She hurried off to take care of some new customers. I admired her firm gate, shapely legs and tiny tennis-shoed feet that served to move her nimbly about. I was adding the numbers up in my head, and concluded that they should put her somewhere near thirty. She didn't look it. It was probably the oriental heritage. Asian women are ageless. Take any four of them in the fourteen to sixty range and you would be hard-pressed to tell which is the granddaughter, grandmother, mother or great-grandmother. Sign that family up for a dish-washing detergent commercial.

As I watched her wait on the table of newcomers, I realized that her father's genes had contributed to her physique. She had full and shapely hips, a tiny curving waist and ample bosom. Definitely a departure from the traditional Asian build; flat chest, no waist and chunky bottom. All in all, a very attractive lady.

I sat and fiddled with my water glass, spinning it around in the condensation from the melting ice that had pooled on the table top. Logic told me to leave a nice tip, give her a smile as

I left and hum a tune all the way back to my room. Something else kept me staring at my hand as it twirled the glass, a full rotation with each spin. It kept spinning until she came back over.

"I hope I'm not being too forward," I said as I tried to stand up casually, "but I was wondering if you might like to show an out-of-towner around this evening."

"Are you staying here?" she asked.

"Yeah," I said, fumbling for my room key. I flipped the red plastic fob over to read the room number. "Room 206."

"I get off at 6:30," she said. "Why don't I just pick you up around on that side and we can go by my apartment so I can change. You like Mexican food?"

"Sure," I said. "A little after 6:30 on the south side. I'll be the one wearing the pink carnation."

"I'll find you," she said. I congratulated myself on making a good decision. I marveled at my tremendous charisma and discerning eye halfway back to my room. At that point I remembered that my trip had a primary purpose. Back to the harness.

10

When I got up to my room. I went right to work. I got out the Yellow Pages and began going through the "Auto Parts" and "Tires" classifications. After just a couple of minutes, I struck pay dirt. It was almost too easy. Lubbins Auto Supply, five locations in the Greater K.C. area. I found a pad of Ramada Inn stationary and made some notations about the addresses and locations of the Lubbins stores. I'm familiar enough with the Kansas City area that I could give myself directions to all of them by using the area maps at the back of the book. Lubbins had sprung the extra bucks for the little "location assistance" codes that tie you in to indexed maps, which made finding the places much easier. I called a couple of the stores to see how late they were open. They closed at six.

I put in another call to Linda. She was calmer. She'd found a bottle of wine and it sounded like it had helped. At least she would sleep.

At 6:25, I was down on the street level of the south side of the Ramada, directly below where my room was located. It had stopped snowing and sleeting, but the wind had picked up and my Woolrich parka wasn't quite thick enough to block it out. I probably would have been warmer with the hood up, but this was a first date, as well as a second impression, and I wanted to look casual and rugged. I balanced myself on a concrete parking spacer to avoid the slush in the parking lot.

Penny pulled around the back of the building at about 6:35. I didn't realize it was her until she flashed her headlights at me as she approached. Her car was a Pontiac Fiero, one of those new little mid-engine two-seaters with retractable headlights. It took me back to my days of auto-infatuation—or maybe she did. She pulled up slowly to avoid splashing slush against my feet and legs. Considerate.

"Hi," she said brightly as she moved a package from the passenger seat and I got in. "Been out here long?"

"Long enough," I said, smiling, as I rubbed my hands together.

She gave me a sly, sideways grin and shoved the Fiero into first gear. No apology or excuse, just a grin. I was beginning to like this girl more and more.

The little Fiero made good tracks in the bad footing. The mid-engine displacement helps a lot with traction and balance in cornering, and that always shows up more when the roads are bad. She also drove well, with a good feel for the car and the sloppy pavement.

It took us about twenty-five minutes to make it to her apartment, which was on the second floor of a big old house in what looked like a nice neighborhood. She pulled around back and parked, and we went up a set of outside stairs. They were slippery, and we both came close to losing our footing more than once. She said that the landlord probably wouldn't get any salt on them until morning. I could have told her some interesting things about his liability.

The apartment was a pretty nice setup inside, front-to-back of the entire second floor, living room toward the front, open kitchen in the middle and, I assumed, bedrooms and bath in the rear. Along the wall opposite the door was a large alcove with big paned windows. The ceiling started sloping inward at mid-window, following the roof line, and set into the sloped portion of the ceiling, on either side of the window, were two three-foot by six-foot skylights. A very nice little sitting room or possibly a small dining area, tucked away to the side between the kitchen and living room. But in this particular household it was put to a much better use. Directly in front of the window, under the skylights and spread out across sheets laid over the hardwood floors were the tools of an artist; a large easel, paint trays, palettes, and cans filled with brushes. There were lots of canvases and sketch pads piled around and leaning against the walls in various stages of completion. This was a working studio, not merely set up for purposes of appearance. I was so intrigued by it all that I almost didn't notice the small blond girl reclined on the couch in the living room, off to my left.

"This is my roommate, Barb," Penny said pleasantly, motioning toward her. Barb shot a quick smile our way and turned back to the TV without speaking. I nodded a silent hello at the back of her head.

"Who's the artist?" I asked, shifting my focus back to the studio area.

"I guess I am," Penny said, "or at least I try. Make yourself at home while I change. You want something to drink?" She took my coat and laid it neatly over the back of a chair. I was wearing my gun, so I kept my corduroy blazer on and buttoned. The sleeve was stretched so tight over my cast that I could barely move on that side for fear of popping the buttons. I looked as uncomfortable as I felt.

"I'd take a beer if you've got one."

"I'm sure we've got one," she said as she ducked around a corner into the kitchen area. She emerged seconds later opening a can of Budweiser, handed it to me and went back into the rear of the apartment calling, "I'll be just a minute," over her shoulder.

I drank my beer and looked closely at the artwork in progress. There were a lot of figure studies, charcoal or pencil on drawing paper, and some oil or acrylic paintings on canvas that had evidently emerged from the drawings. It was good stuff. A warmth spread up my neck and face as I realized that the nude figure which was the subject of almost all of the work belonged to Barb, the girl over on the couch. It's a funny feeling to be looking at a picture or drawing or painting of a naked person when they're right there in the same room with you, fully clothed. I'm no prude, but I was embarrassed.

"She's really good," Barb said, looking around over the back of the couch. Her acknowledgment of my perusal only heightened my discomfort.

"She's better than good," I said as I sorted absently through some of the canvases stacked against the wall. I pulled one out of the stack and held it up at arm's length. It was a wide canvas, about four feet, and not very high, maybe sixteen inches. The subject matter was nothing more than a reclining nude Barb on a green drape with a pair of silver ice tongs in one hand and an empty highball glass in the other. The initial effect was rather bizarre, but the longer you looked at it, the more it seemed to be the kind of painting you'd want hanging on your office wall or in your living room. It had a strange but natural quality, not unlike Penny herself; a pleasing combination of seemingly contradictory elements.

Barb had turned back to the television, but I could tell that the facial features and general dimensions of the painting were very accurate in reference to the live figure as I could see it. There on the couch she looked like a spindly young boy dressed up in daddy's big clothes. Her legs, tucked up under her, were all but invisible beneath the heavy, oversized cotton sweater that she wore. The lines in her face and the arms, wrists and hands that protruded from the sleeves of the sweater would lead one to believe that she would be bony and sparse beneath the clothes. But the painting revealed a rich lushness of breast, thigh and soft belly, not to mention a pair of very shapely, very long and very well-muscled legs. I decided that she must have been a runner with a penchant for pasta. As I went through this analysis I also became aware, once again, of my discomfort with the reality of the girl and the representation of the painting. I fumbled through some of the sketches to avoid having to talk to her. The sketches were all very good. Some were still lifes and there were some landscapes, but most were figure studies, and most of those were of Barb, both clothed and sans covering.

I was relieved when Penny emerged through the kitchen. The brown and gold waitress uniform had been replaced by a black jump suit with lots of zippered pockets, shiny fabric inserts, studs and rhinestones, secured tightly at the narrow waist with a flashy silver belt. She looked absolutely smashing.

Penny drove us to an out-of-the-way little Mexican restaurant called Carmalita's, where I was pleased to discover that they served Corona correctly. Ever since Corona had become the popular fad beer among the college and Yuppie crowds, many of the Mexican establishments that had served it for years as "the beer of Mexico" dropped it almost overnight in a sort of reverse-protest against the bastardization of one of their ethnic symbols. An emphatic reaction in the proud Mexican tradition. I had started drinking the stuff on a long weekend in Matamoros several years ago and my palate had become spoiled. The upwardly mobiles and the college kids hadn't discovered it until about a year ago, and now you can order one just about anywhere. The availability made me happy, even if the popularity of the brew for reasons other than for its natural attributes distressed me. But not seriously. I enjoyed my Corona, and Penny a glass of white wine.

The food was great. There were moments of sheer ecstasy when the hot peppers and jalapeno sauce brought tears to my eyes and the rich, pasty mix of beef, beans and flour tortillas settled back in my throat like so many thousands of pure calories on their way to my belly to lie heavily and hum softly. We ate until we were stuffed, but I limited the Coronas to three. Penny nursed her single glass of wine. When they serve a Corona correctly, it comes with a lime slice on the lip of the bottle, held in place by a toothpick or hors d' oeuvre spear. You squeeze the lime into your frosted mug, pour Corona over the lime and juice, and the result is a superb taste experience. When I had three lime slices in the bottom of my mug, I stopped.

The dinner conversation flowed without effort. Food, sports, travel, politics, it seemed that Penny had an informed opinion and sense of humor about almost any subject. She seemed to be surprised by the fact that I was a lawyer, but then I'm fairly used to that reaction. I told her I was in town working on a case, and she apologized jokingly about keeping me away from my legal research. It was like talking to an old friend. She had started college as an art major at LSU. After her second year, she'd become bored and took a job as an architect's assistant in a large firm. That lasted about a year, and then she went to a hair styling school. That training put her onto a new career, which lasted about three years. While she was doing that, she took up art again and finally decided that she should pursue her true calling full time. After almost a year of the starving artist routine, she followed a friend's advice and enrolled in the fine arts program at UMKC in Kansas City. She'd been going there part-time, waitressing, cutting hair and doing a lot of painting for the last couple of years. She and Barb had worked together cutting hair in a salon, and wound up rooming together when they both walked out of romantic involvements and living arrangements at the same time. I tried not to act too interested in Barb, but once you've seen someone who looks like her naked, it's hard not to be intrigued. Penny got support from her folks and didn't mind working, so she was in no big hurry to finish school. Her approach to life was casual and accepting, while at the same time she asserted an aggressive determination that each of us controls the reality around us. When I told her how good I thought her artwork was, she shyly admitted she'd had a couple of shows and sold some pieces from time to time, here and there. I told her I was somewhat of a collector of obscure or as-yet-unknown artist's work, and that I'd really like to take a look at whatever might be for sale. She acted embarrassed, yet I thought she was also pleased. I learned that she spoke Japanese, although she was admittedly rusty, had two brothers and would have had three or four dogs if her landlord didn't have a ban on pets. I found myself feeling something that brought back memories of times long past. I was having fun. I felt alive again. I was enormously attracted to someone very real. It was refreshing and invigorating.

A fat Mexican guy in a traditional costume was making the rounds between tables with a Spanish guitar. He was really pretty good, or maybe the beer and company were making him sound better than he actually was. In any event, we thoroughly enjoyed his rendition of "La Paloma" at our table. When he finished, I tipped him generously, gazed at my lovely date for a few seconds and lifted a nearly empty beer mug toward her.

"Salud," I said, smiling.

"Gochiso-sama," she replied softly, touching her empty wine glass lightly against my mug. We grinned intently at each other in the candlelight for what seemed like an eternity. Neither of us was wanting to go anywhere.

Finally, though I hated to break the mood, I beckoned our waitress and asked for the check. I was, after all, up here on a job. I asked Penny if she'd be interested in helping me out with a research project. She was more than a little curious and interested.

"But no questions," I said, trying to make a game of it, "until later."

She was intrigued, excited and being patient. If my instincts were accurate, I knew the patience wouldn't last very long.

The Fiero needed gas so she pulled it into an Amoco station. After I had finished pumping the gas and charging it on my credit card, she motioned at me with the keys.

"No," I said, "you drive. I think that a car I'm unfamiliar with, sloppy streets and one arm in a cast might lead to disastrous results. Besides, it's a stick. I can't shift very well with this thing." I pointed to my semi-useless arm and got into the car. "I'll navigate."

I pulled out my notes and gave her directions to the first
Lubbins Store. It was around 9:30, a perfect time to find out
what I needed to know.

"So you're not a lawyer," Penny said, fishing.

"Oh, I am," I said. "I kind of get involved in some things
that are a little, um, out of the ordinary."

"I see," she said. "That how you got the broken arm?"

"More or less."

The first three Lubbins locations were easy, uneventful
and dead ends. They were all situated in little strip-centers,
with large glass fronts and office areas in the back. By peering
in the front, and then driving around and looking in the rear
windows, I could be virtually certain that there were no
lights on or activity inside. I was hoping for a real break on
the off-chance that they might be holding the girl in one of
the stores. This time of the evening there would almost certainly be activity going on; feeding, putting down to bed,
changing of the guard or something. But not at the first three
stops.

There was no way Penny was going to participate in such a
strange game without knowing something. As we made our
rounds, I did fill Penny in on some of the details. I painted
the picture in broad strokes, only filling in details where they
were needed to tie things together. She listened intently,
interrupting several times to ask questions or to clarify certain points. Of course, I wound up telling her more that I
intended to. Credit her angling skills. There was a long period of silence after I finished. She pulled into the parking lot
of the third Lubbins location and completely circled the dark
building slowly without either of us saying a word.

"You're an interesting one," she commented as we headed
for the fourth store. She reached over casually and patted the
gun-bulge beneath my jacket. Her hand went down to rest on
the top of the cast on my arm and then to my hand, and she
gave it a quick squeeze before reaching to downshift. A lady
of silence and understanding.

The fourth Lubbins Auto Supply was in a freestanding building on the north edge of Kansas City, Missouri. There was a six-foot chain-link fence running around the lot and salvage parts piled around the back of the building. The front of the building had only one small display window, and I could see nothing but a service counter and dividing wall from there. I went around to the drive-through gate on the side of the building, figured out the double-lap latch and slid the gate open. It took two hands to work the latch, and I had to squat almost all the way to my knees to work my left hand into a position where it could pull back on the top slide so that I could lift the "Y" latch with the other hand. It was a laborious process.

Once in, I closed the gate and picked my way around the dark metal skeletons to the building's backside. The area was not lit by any sort of floodlights, and it was fairly easy to determine that all areas on the inside of the building were dark and quiet. My guard down, I trudged back toward the gate.

Evidently, I made more noise leaving than I had coming in. I heard a low rumble from behind me and off to my right that I thought was a small engine humming at first. When I finally heard the pad-pad of running paws, it clicked in my head and I knew they were dog sounds.

Without turning to look, I broke for the gate, still thirty feet in front of me. Once you've identified a pursuer, turning to confront them can eliminate the option of flight. The split second that it takes to turn and make visual contact can slow you down and freeze you with fear. I put my head down and ran.

I made the gate in plenty of time, with the growling sounds still several yards behind me. As I started to reach for the latch, I realized that I would never get it open before some part of me would be penetrated by sharp teeth. Holding my breath and setting my jaw, I used what momentum I still had going to hoist myself as high up onto the chain link mesh as possible, and I managed to get my good arm looped over the top of the fence. I scrambled my way over just as the dogs reached the fence line. It was pure adrenalin that got me one-armed and panic-stricken over that fence. Once over, I lost all coordination and control. I fell sideways from my straddled position atop the fence all the way to the ground. It was not pretty.

The dogs snarled and spit not ten inches from my face as I lay there feeling stupid. There were two of them, a sleek doberman and a ratty-looking shepherd mix. Both had ample muscle and tooth to do me harm, and seemed more than willing to do so. I lay there for a minute and let them bark while I internally inventoried the aches and pains I was feeling. I determined that the only major problems were a dull ache from underneath the cast on my left arm, and a severe case of damaged pride. Penny had been parked not ten feet from where I lay, a witness to the entire clumsy performance, and now she was kneeling beside me, asking if I was okay.

"Only embarrassed," I groaned as I sat up. She helped me to my feet and then to the car. We both brushed and picked at the mud, grass and snow clinging to my clothing. I pulled a couple of clumps of frozen dirt out of my hair.

"Let's get the hell out of here," I said. The dogs were making an ungodly racket.

The snow was melting in the warmth of the car, leaving me wet in various degrees all over the right side of my body, and I was concentrating on trying to stay warm and fight off the shivers that kept starting as spasms in the muscles of my back and working their way up to eventually rattle my teeth. I was quite a mess and past the point of vanity.

All the way to our last stop, we were both silent and thoughtful. I was also stewing over my stupidity in not taking precautions and doing the things that should be second nature to someone in my line of work. It's dangerous enough even if you're not stupid. I also felt guilty because I felt responsible for Penny who had, after all, been more or less roped into this. The heater made the air in the small car warm and stale. I felt drowsy. Sleep come free me.

"You ever consider changing occupations?" she said finally, breaking the silence and snapping me back into full consciousness. "I mean, this double profession stuff seems to be sort of hard on you. Most of the attorneys I've ever known drive BMW's, play golf or tennis and worry about their stock portfolios. It's not supposed to be a dangerous job."

"You're forgetting that those guys also have hemorrhoids, high blood pressure and therapists. Danger is a relative thing."

"Point well taken," she said.

"Besides," I said, settling back into the contoured bucket seat, "the hero gets the girl." I could see the dashlights reflecting off of her broad smile out of the corner of my eye. Case, you charmer, you.

The last Lubbins location was in another strip center, and was as dark and silent as the others had been. I observed that all the windows could be seen from the parking area, and opted to make my inspection from the car. No sense pushing my luck. I didn't want another dog-and-Casey show.

By the time we wound our way back to the Interstate, I was finally warm clear down, but very tired, my arm and hip hurt and my nerves were shot. Penny didn't ask where to go, she just drove. I half-dozed.

Before I knew it, we were back at the Ramada. She pulled around to the south side, parked the car and said, "Come on," quietly as she got out and came around to my side of the car and eased me out.

I unlocked the door to my room and we went in. I closed the door behind me. I turned to see her standing in the center of the room, smiling, eyes full of warmth. I grinned in response.

"Get over here," she said, holding her arms out. I stepped into her embrace and she went up on her tiptoes to reach my mouth. The kiss was long and slow and we eased our way into it. Soon our clothes were strewn across the floor, bed and chair, the sheets were askew and all of the lights were off except the one over the sink in the bathroom. She had left that one on, closing the door about two-thirds of the way.

She was all supple energy and silken flesh. We romped and played and grunted with effort until we both slipped slowly into a warm rhythmic trance. I found myself floating in her. We both ran and ran until we were spent, and then lay panting against each other. The warm roundness of her hips and shoulders made the most comfortable of resting places, the sharp curve of her narrow waist a natural indentation to cradle my arms. I fell asleep with the warmth of her breath against the small of my throat.

I awoke as she brushed her hair in front of the mirror. She looked no older than nineteen. I admired the firm, round beasts in profile, the large dark nipples still very erect. Another trait from her Asian heritage.

"What time is it?" I mumbled, massaging my eyes.

"Shh," she whispered in a soothing hush. "It's about three. I've got to get home so I can be back here on my shift by 9:00. You go back to sleep."

I watched with pleasure as she dressed and could hear her humming softly to herself every once in a while. She took one more look in the mirror, put the brush into her purse and walked over to sit on the edge of the bed.

"Goodnight, lover," she said softly as she leaned down to kiss me lightly on the lips.

"Night," I said, and hung onto her hand as she stood up. She paused halfway through the door and gave me a small wave. I waved back.

After she was gone, I groaned and got up to dig my contact case out of the shaving kit. Cold, stooped over and sighing relief, I plucked the hunks of plastic out of my eyes. As I fumbled with the contacts, I realized how difficult the normally automatic process seemed to be. Then I remembered the large piece of white plaster on my left arm, and realized why. Funny how your subconscious can completely block out such things when preoccupied with something more important. I hadn't thought of the cast at all since coming back to my room until that very moment. Mind over matter. I plopped the lenses into their respective cups and climbed back into bed. My throat went "mmmmm" as I pulled the cold sheets up around me and nestled into the pillow. My last sensation before dropping off to sleep was the smell of Penny's perfume on the pillowcase against my face.

11

I woke up with gray light in my eyes, leaking in through the slit between the blackout curtains at the window. I could feel a delicious grin on my face and, I didn't need to look in the mirror to verify my suspicion that I looked absolutely sappy.

I'm too old and tired to spend much time chasing after women. I'd had my share of encounters, relationships and fiascoes before I got married, and then had known the pleasure of that one great love. It had always torn me up that Annie and I wound up unable to live together, when we loved each other so much. Since the divorce, I'd had very little occasion to be with a woman. This one would stay with me for a long time. I could already tell that the memory of Penny was indelibly etched in the sweet-warm places of pure thought that creep up on me in moments when I am truly relaxed. Right now, however, she had left me feeling giddy and boyish and spry. I reveled in the feeling.

The red numbers on the bedside clock radio glowed 9:28 at me, and I convinced myself that I had to get up. Perry would be waiting down at the restaurant for me at ten o'clock. I felt a small sinking feeling as I realized that Penny would be on her shift by ten. Maybe it was anticipation at seeing her. Maybe it was that same feeling I'd experienced for the first time as I rode the bus to school in the fifth grade, in terror of facing Becky Turner when I got there. Maybe it was concern over what Penny might think when she saw me with my cousin Perry. One of the reasons I'd always figured him for mob connections was that he looked the part. Right out of Central Casting, one Mafioso type, please. Maybe I was wrestling with a combination of all those emotions.

I got up and called Linda. She was better, calmer, bored and she had a hangover. At least it took her mind off of things. Well, maybe.

By the time I had showered and dressed it was 10:10, and I hurried downstairs. I found myself standing in front of the entrance to the restaurant, half looking for Perry and half hoping I would spot Penny first. I was experiencing that uncomfortable division of energies that comes with trying to focus your attention on too many things at once. I rubbed my hand over my anxious eyes and tried to concentrate on the business purpose of my visit. It didn't work, so I dealt with first things first. As soon as I had scanned all of the brown uniforms in sight and ruled out the possibility of any of them being Penny's, I was able to spot Perry at a table against the window. Life is tough, Casey, but let's see if we can't deal with these simple things a little more effectively, huh?

It had been about three years since I had seen Perry last, and he'd put on quite a bit of weight. He now looked like an over-inflated Al Pacino rather than the spindly Italian boy I had grown up with. My mother's sister Susan left the family home in Missouri when she was sixteen to find her fortune in New York City. She got as far as New Jersey and was back in four years with what turned out to be her fortune indeed, Frank Cabelli. He was five years older than Sue. They had come out to Kansas City so that Frank could help run a construction company which his brother had started there. My family had joked for years about Uncle Frank being in the Mafia, as if the appearances were only circumstantial, and I think everyone hoped that they belied the truth. Ultimately, no one really cared because Frank was a good father and husband, he and Sue had been relatively successful in raising at least two of their three children, were always loving and inclusive to the rest of the family and Frank's name was clean as a whistle.

Perry had never actually worked for his father. That's what really made me think he'd gone "over the line," if there is such a thing. His dad wouldn't stand for or didn't choose to use the type of employee that Perry wanted to be. But Perry had a name he could capitalize on, and that led him to the connections he needed to get what he wanted.

"So, young James, you wanted to talk?" Perry puffed smoke at me between long drags on his cigarette. There were no less than six dead butts in the ashtray in front of him. He addressed me in the same sort of condescending mockery that he had used when he was ten and I was seven. It still irritated me.

"That'll kill you, you know," I said, motioning toward the ashtray.

"I know, I know," he said, shaking his head. "I quit two, maybe three times a year, but it always starts again. So you've come here to check up on my health?" His wording and intonation sounded so much like they came out of a bad gangster movie that it was almost funny, except that they were so natural and unpretentious that it was kind of scary.

"I need a little help, Perry," I said. "The kind of help I think you can give me. The kind of help neither one of us wants anyone to know you gave me. I'm working for a private party. There's no law involved on my end." Perry gazed at me through expressionless squinted eyes, drawing on his cigarette, and said nothing. "A guy named Paul Matasseren is in jail down in Wichita. They nailed him on a drug thing, but missed the big action that was supposed to come down. They ended up with next to nothing on him. Some folks who thought it might put some pressure on him grabbed his six-year-old kid as leverage for the location of the coke. He doesn't give a shit about the girl. I'm trying to find her."

"This Matasseren guy your client?" Perry asked through the veil of smoke.

"No, the mother. They think she knows where the stuff is, but she doesn't."

He was silent and thoughtful for a minute.

"I know I owe you one," he finally said. "You went way out on a limb for me a couple of years ago. Hey, no one up here would touch me, the word was out to stay back and let me burn. You know, I'm still usin' that Perkins pal of yours. He's a good rep."

I didn't respond. I knew he was talking more to himself than to me.

"Okay, I know a little about the situation," he said, waving his hand toward me as if he were making a concession. "It's a tough one and there's a lot of pressure on from a lot of different directions. Now, I'm not involved at all in any of this, but I can do some checking. You gotta understand that I'm gonna be sticking my freakin' neck out so somebody can louse up my head, and I hope you appreciate that. I'll let you know what I find out if I'm still talkin'." I knew the dramatics were overstated, but the message they were designed to send was loud and clear: our scorecard's even after this one, Coz.

"There's just one catch," I said. "I've got to move, one way or the other, before noon Friday."

"Deadlines, deadlines," he said, shaking his head as he put out his cigarette in the overburdened ashtray. Little bits of ash spilled over the rim and onto the tabletop. I amused myself once again with the irony of the word "deadline" in the context of this situation, but didn't share my dark humor with Perry. He was a humorless kind of guy.

"I can give you a couple of names, if it helps," I said. He nodded. "Wiley or the Wiley brothers, of United Suppliers Tire Warehouse, and Lubbins of Lubbins Auto Supply. Dallas people." He nodded again.

I gave him my room number on the back of a paper napkin. He said he'd get back to me as soon as he could. I told him to leave a message at the desk with a number where I could reach him if I was out when he called.

"Your Aunt Susan sends her love," he said as he stood up from the table. "She said she hasn't seen you since the funeral, that it's been too long. She said to come around if you get a chance."

"Thanks," I said. "The same back to her." I started to hold back the next thought, but then went ahead with it. "Tell her I'm sorry, but there's no time for visits this trip. You know, your mother's a special lady, Perry."

"Hey, she's my Ma, you know?" Perry said, buttoning his coat and looking at something far away out the window.

My mother's sister was indeed a special lady in many respects. If for no other reason in the world, she was special to me because she was so much like my mother. Her face, her carriage, her mannerisms, her voice. Especially her voice. It was no accident that I had not been to visit Aunt Susan and Uncle Frank since my mother's funeral, despite several invitations. I knew that the encounter would be a painful one, that Aunt Susan's visage would be like a haunting, tormenting memory for me; one that would leave me hurting, confused, frustrated and twisting in the wind. I was not ready for that sort of emotional ordeal at this point in my life.

I sat and drank coffee for a few minutes after Perry was gone. A suspicion that had developed during our conversation was now confirmed. I had accounted for all brown uniforms serving in all areas of the restaurant, and Penny's attractive lines were in none of them.

Annie used to tell me that I centralized the world around myself, that I always assumed that any action or reaction that directly affected me was designed or intended to achieve the resulting impact that it had on me. I never allowed for the possibility that things in this world happened for reasons other than to happen to me. I seemed to be doing it again. I felt a painful stab of self-doubt prompted by Penny's absence. She was avoiding me, sending a message of rejection that was all too clear. She couldn't stand the thought of facing me today, while I had been in breathless anticipation of that moment. It was simply too much of a coincidence that she might have taken sick, that her car wouldn't start or that she had simply overslept. Not a chance.

I wandered back to my room feeling sorry for myself. I punched the radio on and milked little bits of melancholy memory out of the songs on the airwaves of WKSR that morning. I chuckled to myself several times as I collected pieces of clothing from some very unlikely places around the room. The word "insecurity" kept popping into my head. I wallowed in the misery of my post-coital depression. We're all entitled from time to time. Billy Joel sang that some love is just a lie of the heart, the cold remains of what began with a passionate start. I commiserated.

I pulled my gym bag from the shelf above the hanging rack just outside the bathroom and began to sort through my arsenal and equipment, spreading them out on the bed. I had brought along plenty of heavy dark clothing and two guns, thus was my armor and artillery. I retrieved my Browning 9mm automatic in the clip holster from the floor next to the bedside table, and pulled a brown leather shoulder holster with an ammunition pouch that held an extra clip for the Browning from inside the bag. The other weapon was in the trunk of my car, where it spends most of its time. It is a black 12-gauge Mossberg pump-action shotgun with a pistol-type grip that rests in a corny green camouflage case wedged under the spare tire and jack. To tell the truth, if you ignore the stupid canvas case, it's a menacing, evil-looking instrument, and I was surprised as hell to be able to walk into a Service Merchandise Store and buy it right over the counter. Its molded, black rubberized stock grip and pump lever combined with the oily black sheen on its metal surfaces make it look like something out of a Mad Max movie, but the sleek barrel is just long enough to be legal, so you can charge one of those babies up on American Express if you're so inclined. It rarely leaves the trunk of my car, but it is comforting at times to know that it's waiting there with its five shells filled with double-aught buckshot at the ready.

I looked at the piles of clothing and meager weaponry on the bed and shook my head slowly. It looked like an issue of "L.L. Bean meets Handgun Hobbyist." I was truly not prepared to take on any sort of organized group that had anything more than a fleeting interest in keeping their hands on the Matasseren girl or finding the drugs. I fought off the tight feeling of panic in my throat and the rush of heat that tried to crawl up my neck and cheeks by telling myself that the grim reality of the situation was the only thing that gave me any advantage at all. They probably weren't afraid of me. I was terrified of them. Apathy was my ally.

I repacked my gym bag, leaving the shoulder holster and a pair of heavy leather work gloves out on the chair in the corner. I flipped on the TV and was thinking about how nice a little nap might feel. A rerun of "The Dating Game" was reminding me of why I made it a personal policy to never watch daytime television. The laughter and applause became a droning hum and I felt myself slipping into the fuzzy warmth of sleep. I was startled awake by the phone, and a glance at the clock revealed that almost two hours had slipped by between the edges of consciousness. I struggled to shake loose the cobwebs of daytime sleep as I answered. It was Perry.

"Those names out of Dallas got me some reactions and some info," he said. "I don't know how they bring the stuff in, but there's a guy here in K.C. who's heavily involved. Name is Joe Freeman. He runs a big sporting goods supply outfit, wholesale to all the high schools, colleges and pro teams with lots of retail outlets in about a six-state area. Name of the operation is Continental Sporting Goods."

"Thanks, Perry," I said.

"Hey, don't thank me," he said quickly. "Nothing to thank, you never even talked to me." He hung up. I wondered which old movie he'd pulled that cliché out of.

I went quickly to my favorite resource, the friendly Yellow Pages. It's absolutely amazing how useful the information in

those little ads can be. "Sporting Goods—Wholesale" led me
directly to Continental Sporting Goods and Supply, "the Midwest's largest supplier of sporting goods and equipment."
Area reps were listed for Missouri, Kansas, Nebraska, Iowa,
Oklahoma and Colorado. Two local office numbers at a downtown address were listed, along with a warehouse number
and separate address. That one intrigued me.

They had not paid extra for the benefit of the locater
index, so it took me awhile to sort through the maps in search
of Republic Avenue, and then to trace it across several maps
until I could cross-reference the street number with another
listing at about the same address. I finally found an equipment rental business on a cross street within a few blocks,
and used their locater index to find the right map. Much
harder than calling and asking for directions, but easier than
having to make up a cover story or having someone remember my voice. I put an "X" on the map at about where the
Continental Warehouse should be and tore that page out of
the book. They'd never miss it. I jotted the phone numbers
and addresses from the ad down on a piece of Ramada Inn
stationary and stuck them, along with the map, in the pocket
of my shirt.

I had the whole afternoon to look, so I took a crosstown
route to the area encompassed by my map. I found Republic
Avenue and stopped inside the north edge of the area to
orient myself. I was in an industrial/warehouse zone, with
train tracks running between and among the large warehouses six and eight abreast. This area must have been something to see in the heyday of rail transport. There was lots of
truck traffic and little in the way of pedestrians. It gave me
comfort to note that no one was really taking notice of me. I
headed on down Republic about six blocks and saw a sign on
the front of an old red-brick warehouse that said "Continental Sporting Goods." There was one small door in the front,
and I guessed that there would be loading docks in the rear.
The docks opened out onto a wide expanse of concrete with

railroad tracks criss-crossing it and two wide alleyways for truck traffic along the backs of the opposing buildings. The Continental building had four large metal overhead roller doors, with a man-sized access door on the rear end, next to a set of metal stairs, and another set of similar double doors on the far end of the docks. There was loading and unloading activity between two of the overhead doors and an unmarked tractor trailer rig parked along the platform.

I cruised by slowly, trying not to look conspicuous, and made mental measurements of the building and the surrounding areas. Then I wound my way out of the complex of old warehouses, climbed up on the Interstate and headed back toward the Ramada.

As I buzzed along with the traffic at seventy-two miles per hour, a red Fiero passed me in the right lane. I pulled up until I was about even with the rear bumper, glanced down and noticed that I had sped up to about eighty, and fixed my eyes ahead as I pulled even with the driver's door. After a couple of nonchalant glances, I could see that the driver was blond, a guy, and about seventeen years old. I pondered over the infathomable number of red Pontiac Fieros there must be in the Kansas City area. How wide the ocean? How high the sky? As I thought great thoughts and let my mind wander in philosophical contemplation of the universe, a more earthly and pertinent thought occurred to me. I dug the piece of paper with addresses and phone numbers scrawled on it from my pocket and unfolded it. I had a little time and more than a little curiosity.

Continental's "executive officers" were supposed to be in a downtown high-rise, but a note taped to the grubby door said that the offices had moved to the Eberhardt Plaza Office Suites, and gave directions. It took me about twenty-five minutes to get there. The new headquarters were very impressive and more than a notch or two above the quality of the previous location.

Eberhardt Plaza was one of those glass-and-cedar complexes, semi-circular around its own man-made lake. The high ticket offices had big full wall windows looking out onto the carefully maintained landscaping that surround the lake. It all looked a little bit too green for that time of year.

The parking area went all the way around the outside of the complex, and I wound my way around behind what was designated as building "four." I took a swift, silent elevator to the third floor.

Huge double oak doors with carved insert panels and a brass plaque bearing the Continental name opened up into a large plush reception area. The lighting was muted and directional, the carpet thick and plush and the walls paneled in the same heavy oak as the doors. Business must be good. An oak counter curved out from the wall to the left of the doorway. A petite girl with short dark hair struggled with a typewriter ribbon at the desk level platform behind the counter. I leaned up against the big curve of oak and bumped it lightly with my cast, on purpose.

"Oh, I'm sorry," said the girl, looking up from the typewriter. "I didn't hear you come in. Can I help you?" She shifted very easily from her frustrated face to a startled look and eventually to the practiced smile of a receptionist.

"Is Mr. Freeman in?" I asked, trying my best to give her my casual but charming smile. I can do it if I try.

"I believe he's in the building somewhere," she said. "Can I tell him who's calling?"

"James Casey," I responded. "You might tell him that I represent Linda Matasseren."

She poked around on a very complicated looking phone, making several hushed inquiries followed by precise little punches on the keyboard. She finally hung up and told me cheerily that Mr. Freeman would be up in a couple of minutes, if I didn't mind waiting. As soon as I nodded and headed for a chair, her pliable face shifted into focused consternation as she dove back into the crippled typewriter. I could hear little grunts and shuffles from behind the counter as she wrestled with the machine and I sunk into the textured velour softness of one of those heavily padded box chairs that have become very popular in office reception areas and night clubs. I never know where to put my arms. The sides are so high that you nearly dislocate your shoulders getting them up there, and you feel like you're in a straitjacket if you wedge them in at your sides. I crossed my legs and hooked my intertwined fingers over my right knee as best I could with a cast on my arm. A compromise.

Joe Freeman came bursting in after about five minutes, swinging both heavy oak doors open forcefully from the middle. He was fiftyish, of average build and height and wore a black Stetson. His hard, round belly and barrel chest stuck prominently out over his western belt and big silver buckle. He had on a well-worn leather vest, open at the front, over a thick wool shirt with the sleeves rolled up to his elbows. His Stetson was flecked with bits of ice and snow, as were the thick sideburns and beard that formed a fuzzy gray-black frame for his ruddy face. He'd obviously been working outside. His wide-wale cords had a sharp but casual crease, and they broke just the right amount over his lizard-skin boots. You can always spot a guy that wears a lot of cowboy boots. In order to get the pants to break correctly, they must be hemmed with a front-to-back taper, to follow the steep contour of the boot. Otherwise, the pants look either too long or too short. It must have been my week for cowboys.

"Debbie, we'll be in my office, no calls, please." His voice was gruff, but the intonation and diction signaled education and sophistication. A cowboy with some class.

"C'mon," he said without looking at me as he walked past. I struggled up out of the chair and followed him down a corridor behind Debbie's counter to a big, dark office. Boxes, both opened and sealed, covered much of the floor space. A pile of shoulder pads, ten or fifteen pair high, stood in a corner. The guest chairs and a small table between them were covered with an assortment of football helmets, soccer balls and brightly-colored nylon jerseys. A group of golf clubs and baseball bats leaned against the front of the desk. The desk itself was buried under a dome of papers in disarray. It was not a neat office, but was very richly appointed beneath all the junk.

He shoved his hand behind the pile of equipment on one of the chairs, swept it onto the floor and said, "Sit." It was not an order, more like a statement. I sat. He went around behind the desk, swiveled himself into the high-backed leather chair and pulled a cigar from a humidor retrieved from under a huge pile of papers. He looked like the cigar type. He didn't offer me one, but took his time lighting his and then finally, for the first time, looked me in the eye.

"Now what the fuck is this shit about the Matasseren broad?" The intonation and diction were gone. If he intended to throw me off balance with the foul language and shift in attitude, he succeeded momentarily. I was actually more taken aback by the fact that he didn't mickey-mouse around feigning ignorance about the situation. He came right at me.

"Mrs. Matasseren has retained me to represent her with regard. to any involvement she may eventually have in her husband's arrest," I said. It was pure horseshit. I needed some scramble time to get my feet back under me.

"You're a lawyer?" Freemen asked, leaning forward to look at me with one raised eyebrow. His tone was challenging and full of disbelief. His gravelly voice came at me in a solid, even monotone. He moved the cigar from his mouth between two heavy fingers that had coarse, dark hair on the knuckles, the hand swinging away from his lips on a thumb that pivoted against the end of his broad chin. Smoke enveloped his face, hand and upper arm as he exhaled slowly. It all had kind of a mystical effect due to the overhead lighting created by a big skylight in the high ceiling. I suddenly realized that I was being intimidated. Successfully. The thick hand swung the cigar back into the waiting mouth, rotating at the wrist, without any shift in position.

"Yup," I said, in answer to his question. I wanted to let him do all the talking. He didn't seem to feel the need to hold back on my account.

"Okay, so tell me what the fuck you want or get the hell out," he said through the thick cigar smoke. So much for my strategy. Scramble time was over.

"I think you might have some information that could be helpful to my client," I started out cautiously. "She is receiving a lot of pressure regarding her knowledge about her husband's illegal activities. She thinks that you could verify the fact that she has no such knowledge." I was really out on a limb, but I had to get some sort of reaction out of him to be able to read him, one way or the other.

"That's crap," he said. "That woman doesn't know me. Hasn't ever heard of me. I know that for a fact." His manner was of total confidence. Hard to rattle. I wondered how Harry O. would have handled this one.

"She'd also like to get her daughter back," I said after a few moments of silence. I watched carefully for any reaction. I saw it. It was nothing you would catch in the normal casual conversation. It was no more than a brief momentary bulge that appeared between his eyebrows. It didn't even create a furrow, just a tiny tensing of muscle between skin and skull. But it was there.

"You're a person that could get hurt, Mr. Casey," Freeman said. The more refined speech pattern had returned. "That sounded something like an accusation. People who make unfounded accusations are always in danger. I know Paul Matasseren. I know he has a wife and daughter. I don't know anything more about either of them. Besides," he said with a malicious twinkle in his eye, "we have already recovered Mr. Matasseren's, ah, property." He leaned back heavily into his chair and drew deeply on his cigar. End of discussion, case dismissed.

"Thank you for your time, Mr. Freeman" I said, rising. I turned and walked from the office, closing the door behind me. I fought off an intense desire to break into a run all the way to the car. I could hear the hornets buzzing behind me. I didn't look back. I didn't know what I'd accomplished. I wasn't sure what I'd been trying to accomplish. It's hard to tell whether you've been successful or not under those circumstances. Buzz, buzz.

12

As I drove carefully back toward the motel I wrestled with the new pieces of the puzzle Freemen had given me. If what he had said about locating the drugs was true, they would have no reason to continue to hold the girl. They would also have no reason not to kill her. He could also be bluffing about having the drugs, but there'd be no real benefit in that to him, since he had to know I was looking for them too. He could use me as a bloodhound to lead them to the stash, if I found it first. Did he or didn't he have the drugs? Did he or didn't he have the girl? The weight of the questions pulled on me like an overabundance of gravity. I felt a heavy reluctance to go over fifty-five. I gazed warily at the cars passing me on both the left and right. Joe Freeman had left me feeling small, alone, in danger, and, in short, incredibly vulnerable. I imagined that he had a similar effect on quite a few people. Maybe this surge of vulnerability brought me to a heightened awareness of potential dangers, but right then and there on the Interstate was the first time that I noticed the silver gray Plymouth following behind me.

Something in the back of my mind told me that I'd seen it there sooner, hanging back in my rear-view mirror, a little too far away for the traffic pattern or with a couple of cars between us, but I'd been too careless or preoccupied to let it register. As I watched in the mirror I could see two silhouettes in the car, both of them male, and I tried to remember specifically where or even if I might have seen the car before, but I couldn't pin anything down. Maybe it was only paranoia, but the silver sedan gave me an overwhelming feeling of déjà vu. My subconscious told me that it had been hanging

around back there ever since I'd hit K.C. I pulled off the
Interstate and into a nearby Quik-Trip. From inside, I
watched as the Plymouth cruised by slowly on the far side of
the gas pumps, pulled back out onto the street and sped off
toward the east. I jumped quickly into my car and headed in
the opposite direction, winding my way down several side
streets to another access ramp onto the Interstate. I drove
directly back to the Ramada with a gnawing feeling inside my
chest. I knew it wasn't hunger or angina. I felt better once I
had reached my room and locked myself in. Refuge.

Suddenly, the gnawing feeling became a sharp wrenching
pain that grabbed my stomach and made my forehead grow
uncomfortably warm and moist. Penny. If someone had been
following me, and doing an even halfway decent job of it,
they would have tracked me to her apartment. She had never
shown up for her shift that morning as far as I knew. My mind
raced back to the previous evening, trying to summon up
some recollection of a car behind us as we drove around to
the Lubbins locations, an oddly-parked vehicle across the
street from us when we stopped or a passing car on an
otherwise untraveled street. I drew a blank.

Then I remembered one small incident that had lodged
itself somewhere back in my pea brain as being slightly out of
order. When we had been in the Mexican restaurant a guy in
a suit and overcoat had come in off the street, glanced around
the entire eating area, his eyes settling on several tables,
including ours. He exchanged a few words with the girl at the
cash register, smiled and laughed a little, bought a mint from
a basket on the counter and left. He was too old to be the
girl's boyfriend. Very strange. How many people drop in to a
restaurant just to chat? On a miserable, cold night when the
quick dash from car to building was hardly worth it? I could
feel my heart pumping in my chest as I tore through the
phone book looking for Penny's number. I looked under all
the "Reynolds" listings. No initial "P's," Pennys or Penelo-
pes. I had no idea what her street address was. "Penny"

could be a nickname or might come from her middle name as far as I knew. The phone could be registered to Barb, and I hadn't even the slightest notion of her last name. A sickening helpless feeling settled over me. I pitched the phone book through the open bathroom door and laid back on the bed. I closed my eyes. I'd had my head up my ass since the beginning of this little caper, and it was affecting too many of the people around me. I was becoming a danger to myself and all those whose lives I touched. Someone ought to jerk my license or something.

Slowly, logic began to move in and take over. I could go downstairs and get Penny's number from someone on the restaurant staff, but what good could I do her now? If they were going to try to use her as some sort of leverage on me, they had probably already made their move, and if such was the case, any progress I made toward locating Sara would be progress toward helping Penny. Besides, if they were using Penny, they'd have to be making contact with me pretty soon for it to have any effect. There was nothing I could do about it right then, and the anxiety was counter-productive. As cold and unfeeling as it might sound, and as hard as it was to do, I had to put that aspect of the problem out of my mind for the time being and concentrate on the task at hand. I couldn't let a series of imagined events cause me to screw up the rest of this very real situation worse than I already had. Stop the bleeding, cut the losses. All your energies concentrated on the here and now, focus on one reality at a time. Use the Force, Luke. I managed to pull my head together for at least a little while, but my intestines were still tied in knots.

I changed into a heavy dark turtleneck and a waist-length leather bombardier jacket that allowed greater mobility and offered better protection. I switched my gun from the clip-holster on the waistband of my jeans to the shoulder holster and harness, which I strapped on over the turtleneck. The shoulder rig housed the gun more securely under my left arm, and made it a little easier to get at. Concepts like mobility, protection and security sounded good, as I thought about them, but I hoped to myself that there was no reason to consider such things. I kept telling myself that I was changing to be fresh and stylish.

I made another call to Linda. This time our roles seemed to have reversed. She was comforting me. I was still in a state of anxiety over the afternoon's events, and she was watching TV and eating popcorn, life as usual. Her placid attitude had a momentary calming effect on me, but it went away as soon as I hung up the phone. I was going out among the bad guys. I had the jitters.

It then occurred to me that Linda's calm resolve was terribly out of sync with reality. With each passing hour, her child was in more danger. As the clock ticked down on the time we'd been given, our options became more limited and hope dissipated. Why then did she seem to relax more as time passed? I concluded that she must have been in a denial mode as a method of dealing with the pressure of the situation. Either that or she was drinking more. I however, had weightier problems than Linda's psychosis or substance abuse on my mind right then.

I decided that my going without food wasn't doing anyone any good. I went downstairs and checked the restaurant. No Penny, so I opted not to eat there. I drove to a little diner that I had passed earlier on my first trek to the Continental warehouse. It was a "mom-and-pop" operation in the true sense of the word. "Val" took the orders and "Sammy" slung the hash. You could tell they'd been married some thirty-odd years just by their treatment of each other, the unstated messages that passed back and forth, and their age. I sat at the counter and allowed the entertainment to monopolize my attention. The meat loaf and mashed potatoes weren't bad, either.

I was halfway through my dinner when a beat-up old full-size Blazer with no muffler pulled into the small parking lot that belonged to the diner and made a spectacle of four-wheeling around in the slush and over the concrete parking dividers. It finally parked with its big fog lights shining brightly in the front windows of the place, and when the lights dimmed two kids in big down parkas jumped out. They came in noisily, stomping lots of snow and mud from their boots onto the linoleum floor. They were around eighteen years old, with that stupid abandon that is a part of being that age which allows you to look at the world as if it exists only right here and now, and as if there are no such things as consequences or tomorrows. The boys shouted loud obscenities mixed with a demand for immediate service at the owner, referring to him as "Pops." The only patrons in the place other than myself and the newcomers were a middle-aged couple, and they left money on their table and departed in an annoyed rush. The owner was getting frustrated back in the kitchen and his wife was taking a lot of abuse about everything she did or didn't do. I felt the hair on the back of my neck bristle and my cheeks flush in anger. Someone ought to teach these punks a lesson. I could whip out my 9mm automatic and threaten them. They'd probably shit their pants, and it wasn't too good for Sammy's business. I could slide on down the counter until I was sitting right next to them and simply be a silent but intimidating force. I could politely ask them to leave on account of they were ruining my meal and flex my muscles or beat my chest to show them I meant business. Or I could tend to my own affairs, finish my mashed potatoes and let the proprietor of the establishment deal with the situation. I chose the latter course of action. Jay Price would have been proud of me. Despite what he might think I am not gung-ho to get involved in every situation I stumble upon. This one was not to my particular liking or within my area of expertise, and I already had more than my own share of problems to deal with. Besides, boys will be boys.

Val brought them their chili and Cokes and they quieted down to eat. Val and Sammy probably had a lot more experience with this kind of thing than I did, and it seemed that simply ignoring the youngsters was the best way to shut them up. I followed that lead, but decided to stick around nursing a mug of coffee and a piece of pie. The boys left fairly quietly, and even paid, but they made a couple more loud passes across the parking lot on their way out. Just don't run into my car, assholes.

It had started to get dark by the time I'd finished my second mug of coffee. That one made my eighth of the day. I was wired. I trudged out into the brisk air, and felt a few tiny stings on my face from the very light snow that had begun to fall again. It was full darkness by the time I got back to the Continental Warehouse. I parked down the block and across the tracks. It was a wide-open area, with vehicles scattered around all of the buildings, so I wasn't overly concerned about being spotted. I'd positioned myself so that I could see all of the back windows of the building, and even though there was a lot of space that I couldn't see, I figured that I'd at least be able to determine whether there was any activity going on inside. I looked around for the gray Plymouth. It was nowhere in sight.

It was about 7:30, and there were two lighted windows on the second floor of the warehouse, and one right next to the regular access door on the ground floor. I had rummaged around in the trunk and located my binoculars before setting out on my quest, and I thumbed the focus wheel as I gazed through them towards the windows. The magnification was just about right for the distance at which I sat. I could focus in on the windows and doors just as if I were standing on the street right outside the building.

At about 7:45, a dark Oldsmobile Cutlass pulled up to the loading platform where there were concrete stairs running up from the street level. Two bundled-up men carrying sacks got out and huddled against the cold. I watched closely through the binoculars as the driver rapped what looked like three even knocks on the metal access door. The door opened from the inside after a foggy cloud of exhalation hung in front of the driver's face for a second. I guessed that the cloud had been a response to an inquiry from inside. I also guessed that the guy who opened the door had either been waiting for the knock, or had been located in close proximity to the door, since there had only been about two seconds between knock and response. Light from inside spilled out onto the loading platform when the door was opened, and I got a quick glimpse of the door attendant before the two visitors hustled in. Most of what I saw was a red-and-black buffalo plaid shirt.

A couple of minutes later I saw shadows across the second floor windows that were lit. Nothing distinctive, just dark indications of movement. Ten minutes later the two men were back down in their car and driving away.

Doing a lot of conjecture, and reading what I wanted to see into it, I could put together this scene:

There were at least two people inside the building besides the girl. She was probably up on the second floor, in some sort of office or makeshift bedroom. The guy downstairs by the door was on guard duty. Because they had to keep the posts filled all the time, the two men in the car had brought food and/or supplies. Being this far into the evening, they would probably not return until morning. Of course, that was making a lot of assumptions. There could be no girl, no involvement at all, and a very reasonable explanation for the activity. People work late. Projects need watching. Something in my gut, though, told me that I was close. My instincts said the girl was inside. If she wasn't, I would have, at best, an embarrassing situation on my hands, and at worst, a dangerous one.

I decided to let them eat and settle into what had probably become a boring, routine evening by now. If I needed it, I wanted the edge of boredom, listlessness and lazy comfort working my way.

I gave them an hour to eat and relax, and then eased myself out of the car. I slipped on the leather work gloves that

I'd picked up back in my room as I stared at the building through the light snow. I poked the index finger of my right hand through a one-inch slit that I'd cut in that finger of the glove. It was a trick I'd learned as a boy when pheasant hunting in absolutely intolerably cold weather. The slit allows you the luxury of heavy gloves, while still giving you the necessary tactile input to effectively operate the safety release and trigger of a gun. The gloves were good for punching, too, but I was here on a friendly visit, right? That thought sparked an idea, and I paused briefly as I neared the trunk of my car. I was thinking of the Mossberg shotgun in the trunk. It would certainly be a confidence-builder as I went in among these new and impressionable friends. After all, they might have been told to expect me, and I would most certainly want to exceed their expectations. On the other hand, I didn't want to go charging in there like Rambo. I might, after all, be dead wrong about this being the place where the girl was being held. And even if I wasn't wrong, which I didn't happen to think I was, I wanted to try to get in and out with the girl as peacefully and quietly as possible. Somehow the shotgun seemed to work against that goal. The Mossberg stayed in the trunk.

I did, however, pull the Browning automatic out of the shoulder holster and slide the clip out. Holding it up in the reflected light, I could see that it was full. I shoved it back into the grip of the gun with a solid snap, and pumped a round up into the chamber. Making sure the safety was still on, I returned the gun to its holster. Me and the Boy Scouts; always prepared.

As I brushed the tiny snowflakes from my eyelashes, another thought struck me. Maybe I ought to call the boys in blue and ask them to help me out on this mission. Sure, I'd ring them up and say, "Hey guys, how about helping me storm this warehouse up here in north K.C.? We'll go in and rescue this kidnap victim that I forgot to tell you, the Wichita Police and the Feds about. Must have slipped my mind. I've got no real evidence that she's in there, but I figure we'll go in with guns a-blazing and ask questions later. That's the way you guys do it, right? Standard police procedure, no need for search warrants or the like. It'll be fun, guys, how about it?" Let's just say that I figured my chances of recruiting the local police to help me were somewhere on the down side of nil. Besides, getting them involved would probably take all night and a better part of the next day, and the girl would probably end up dead. You're solo on this one, Case.

13

I made my way carefully across the tracks and two expanses of concrete to the stairs. I felt terribly exposed as I walked slowly through the bright areas illuminated by the various security lights mounted on the buildings. I crept up the stairs and hoped for visibility through the window by the door. I leaned flat against the wall on the far side of the window, away from the door, and prayed that no one would come out of the building. I could duck away easily enough into the loading area so as not to be seen by a car turning around the corner of the building, but the door opened toward me, and anyone emerging and spilling light out into the area would be immediately face-to-face with a fully illuminated me.

I turned and leaned slowly into the light of the window and strained to see inside. The wire mesh reinforced glass was partly frosted over, but there was a clear area in the middle. I tried to adjust the focus of my eyes to identify something inside. I finally recognized a curved area of red-and-black check as the door attendant's shoulder. He was facing away from me. More confident with the knowledge of his location, I leaned further toward the clear glass, aware that there might be someone else facing him, and the window. There wasn't. He was seated, about five feet from the window, at a small table. There were Hardee's wrappers and bags scattered across the table. He was nursing a large red mug of steaming coffee from a thermos on the table. To his right, also on the table, was a handgun, resting on its left side, butt to the right, barrel pointing away. Readily available to his grasp, assuming he was right-handed. I watched him quietly as I thought and planned. He sipped his coffee.

135

I hadn't noticed the gun in his hand when he opened the door for the two men earlier, but I had been a long way off with vision restricted by the parameters of the binoculars and clouded by the light snow. It then occurred to me that the window was close enough to the door that I could possibly get a quick peek after knocking. I ducked below the window and stepped carefully between the door and window to try out the distance. About four feet. It was possible.

I unzipped my jacket and reached inside once again to the gun tucked under my arm, just to test its accessibility. My sleeve hung up a little on the zipper, so I unzipped the coat another six inches. I positioned myself, took a deep breath and knocked three solid raps on the door. I jumped quickly to the window just in time to see the plaid shirt move out of sight, and to see the corner of the table empty. We would not be exchanging friendly hellos.

The door startled me as it opened. I had been waiting for some sort of verbal inquiry, based on what I had observed earlier. The other guy must have just chosen to breathe out right at that particular time and I had mistaken the fog of warm air as evidence of speech. Maybe it was part of their routine that no one on their team came after the meal visit, or maybe they always phoned ahead. Maybe they had been expecting me, lying in wait. In any event, I was unprepared. My gun was still nestled snugly in its warm holster beneath my jacket. I wondered to myself why I didn't have it out before I even knocked. There is no explanation for stupidity.

I almost didn't react in time, and he had his gun up and pointed at waist level as he leaned out with the swing of the door. Fortunately, he was looking forward rather than over the side where I stood. I braced against the wall and kicked the door away from me with the flat of my foot. He had a firm enough grip on the knob that it jerked him off balance and he started to fall forward, raising both arms to catch himself. I helped his fall along by bringing both hands, clasped to-gether, down from over my head onto his back, right between the shoulder blades. The cast added weight and substance to the blow. His foot caught on the raised metal doorsill and he went down into a kneeling position. I heard a metallic grinding sound as the gun hit the concrete beneath his hand and bore his weight. He bellowed in pain and surprise as my big hiking boot came down on the back of his hand. As my foot slipped off to the side, his hand jerked back, leaving the gun in the slush. I fell slightly forward as my weight tried to shift and I leaned against the door, which had reached its stop, holding it perpendicular to the building. Plaid Shirt had continued the backward motion started with the retreat of his hand and had now rocked back into a squatting position just behind the doorsill. His left hand clutched his right hand and he looked at me for the first time, a look of surprise and annoyance, but not of fear. That froze me for a moment. I swung a heavy boot at the general area of his knees, toward his hands, but my split second of hesitation had given him an edge. He jumped back and sprung into a crouch, all in the same motion. The momentum of my missed kick carried me inside the door and I spun hard against the inside wall to steady myself and then turned back around to face him. He missed an opportunity as I pushed off the wall and planted my feet. As I steadied and faced him he remained in the half-crouch, rubbing his hand.

I barely noticed the movement as he let his hands fall to his sides, but a reflection off the shiny metal brought my eye to the blade that had appeared in his right hand. He held the knife close to his leg, palm up, fingers curled loosely around the handle.

I knew that I had to take the initiative. I also knew that I wouldn't have many moves. Going for my gun was out of the question. Plaid Shirt was too close and potentially too quick to risk that kind of motion. He would slice me like a piece of pumpkin pie before I had my hand on the grip. I knew that I didn't have much time before he would come at me, taking the offensive. Instinct took over.

When I was in high school, there was an Oriental kid who had come right off the boat, so to speak, from Thailand, who transferred into our school at mid-semester. He spoke very little English, but was so innately intelligent that he mainstreamed right into our all-English curriculum and picked up the language very rapidly on his own. He was in a couple of my classes, including gym. We arrived at an arrangement one day after school when I saw him working out. He would teach me the basic moves and combinations of the Thai martial arts, which he had been practicing in the gym that day, and I would teach him to swim. He taught me several sets of moves and a series of routines to practice for keeping the reflexes in tone. I never learned any of the formal crap that goes along with the discipline or even the names of the moves or fighting style. I did learn the routines pat, however, and practiced them until I could make the moves almost unconsciously. I later thought of my Thai friend on more occasions than I am comfortable with, thanking him every time for helping me to build the automatic skills into my system which have saved my butt from one danger or another. This was another such time.

I closed the distance between Plaid Shirt and myself with two brisk steps. He instinctively leaned backward, but stood his ground, the knife waving back and forth in front of his right knee. I stood just beyond striking distance, either with his knife or my long arms. I realized for the first time that I had about three inches of height on him and a lot of reach. He was probably right in my weight class, though, built like the proverbial fireplug.

My left knee rose up to just above waist level, with the lower leg pointed straight down. This motion serves as both a distractor and a counterbalance for leverage. As he adjusted his body to what looked like a kick coming from my left leg, my right foot left the floor in a similar motion, but the lower leg began pivoting upward on the knee hinge from the moment it left the floor. Briefly airborne, with the left leg pro-

viding leverage and momentum, the right foot can whip upward at an incredible velocity, ending its split-second of
travel in a nasty snap at the peak of its arc. When aimed and
timed correctly, this whipping motion focuses all of its de-
structive energy into the throat and lower jaw of your target.
The fact that I wore a four-pound Vasque cured-leather, lug-
soled climbing boot on my foot made the maneuver more
impressive and effective. One of the things my friend Kwan
had taught me was that the legs are much longer, heavier and
stronger than the arms. As a result, with the proper mobility,
the legs make a much more formidable weapon than the
traditional barrage of fists. Add a shoe or well-weighted boot
to the formula and it's like punching with an iron boxing
glove. Of course, the arms and hands are still important, but
in this particular fighting style they serve mainly in a supple-
mentary or defensive role.

My aim was accurate enough, but Plaid Shirt was faster
than I had given him credit for. The kick caught him squarely
under the jaw, slamming his head back and making a crack-
ing sound against his throat. He was out before he hit the
floor, but not before he had managed a sideways slash of the
knife blade that tore an ugly rip in my leather jacket underneath the left arm, just below the level of my lowest rib. It
did similar damage to my body, and I became immediately
aware of the fast, warm flow of blood down my side and leg
beneath my clothes.

I stumbled toward ol' Plaid, who had fallen back into some
boxes and was slumped against the wall. It startled me to see
the knife laying beside him with my own blood on it. There
were several red welts on his neck, and his jaw was misshapen and swelling quickly. Blood ran from the corner of his
slack mouth. He looked as if he would be out of it for a while.
I untucked his shirt and used the knife to cut off most of the
left front panel to use as a bandage. I knew that I needed to
get something on my wound to slow down the bleeding, but I
didn't have much time since he'd made such a racket when

he fell against the boxes, which in turn had toppled noisily against some metal shelves. Whoever was upstairs would be wondering what the noise was all about.

I pulled off my jacket, aware that my whole left side was beginning to numb. "What the hell," I thought, "I can't use the left arm anyway." I wadded the piece of shirt, pressed it against my perforated side and pulled Plaid Shirt's belt from around his waist. His limp body made things difficult, but the thick leather belt finally slid loose. He was bigger around the middle than me so the belt fit snugly around my mid-torso on the last buckle hole. The whole procedure was maddeningly slow because I had to do it with one hand, and the cast was in my way. The white plaster was stained with blood on the bottom and back. The finicky resident at the hospital in Dallas would probably have been upset with me. Temporary repair complete, I set out to find a way to the lighted room on the second floor that I had seen from the outside. Even with the makeshift direct-pressure bandage in place, I was aware that I was losing blood. Just one more factor that sort of put a rush on things.

It took me awhile to find the stairway without turning on any lights, but I didn't want to give the people or person on the second floor any more warning than they already had that I was on my way. As I made my way up the dark stairway, I heard the phone ringing back on the table at Plaid Shirt's post. It stopped abruptly. Maybe someone had picked up an extension. I had my gun out now, poised in my right hand, barrel pointed up, about ten inches from my right shoulder, safety off. I listened to the sound of my knees creak and pop as I ascended the dark and otherwise silent stairwell. I should have been an accountant. Sitting at a desk all day hammering on a calculator is better on your knees than this crap, and you rarely need to carry a gun. Well, maybe around April 15th of each year.

I shifted the gun to my left hand for a few seconds, keeping it in the raised, ready position as much as my cast would allow, while I removed the heavy glove from my right hand with my teeth, one finger at a time. Now that I was relatively sure that the girl was somewhere within, and I was injured, I was not going to put on any airs about doing battle. It was time to be armed and dangerous. The glove leather left a tart, dirty taste in my mouth, and I moved my tongue across the back of my teeth and swallowed frequently as I stuffed the glove into the back pocket of my jeans and moved the gun back into my right hand. The metal was cold against my warm, wet palm.

As I emerged from the open stairway onto the second floor, I could see light coming from an office area off to the left. It looked like there were several offices, all with plate glass windows looking out into the warehouse area. Light spilled out of the third window down the row.

I moved cautiously along in front of the unlit offices toward the closed door of the lighted one. As I stood directly in front of the dark window of the second office, I heard an explosion that sent me falling and diving off to the right out of sheer reflex. I crunched and tumbled through a shower of broken glass as I rolled into a squatting position. I turned back toward the office just in time to see a flash and to hear the distinctive bark of a handgun. I heard the "hiss-plunk" of the slug as it echoed into the darkness behind me. Someone was shooting at me. I dove behind the protection of a wall that partitioned off a section of the storage area. I could see a light switch on the wall above me in the reflected glow of the light from the office. I reached up and flipped it on. I was better off with light, since the other person doing the shooting was probably familiar with the layout of the place, and I wasn't. Big overhead fluorescent lights flickered on and froze some movement over by the doorway of the second office. As my eyes were drawn to the moving shape, I could see that it was Arnie Moore, my favorite glass-breaker and long-time buddy from the two incidents earlier in the week, and he had the girl. I could tell by the way he was looking around that he didn't know where I was.

Maybe Moore wasn't as dumb as he looked. He had evidently been lying in wait for me in the darkened second office, while using the lit third one as a decoy to draw me right past him. As I moved by the big window, he had an easy shot through the glass at me, with a backup second shot out in the open floor of the warehouse. Fortunately for me, he had missed both chances. He must have flunked the marksmanship course at thug school.

He was backed against the door frame of the office with his right hand holding a gun across the girl's small chest at about his own knee level. With his left hand, he grasped a wad of hair from the back of her head and pulled on it sharply whenever she tried to move. She sobbed uncontrollably, her eyes unfocused and filled with tears that ran in a steady flow down her cheeks onto her dress. Every time Moore jerked her by the hair, a spattering of tears would fly from her face and fall to the floor. Both of her hands were raised up to her mouth and she gnawed and slobbered on the fingers as they pulled at her lips and cheeks. She had wet her pants, and the dirty white tights she had on under the dress were stained a fresh yellow-gray from up under the hemline to the insides of her knees. She looked very different from the girl in the picture that was in the pocket of my jacket.

"Step out into the open, or I'll kill the kid," Moore said, digging the side of his gun into the girl's sternum. His eyes darted randomly around the darkened and concealed areas of the large room. "Don't try any funny stuff, I'll do it!"

I eased myself slowly around the corner out into the open, leading the way with my gun, which I held at eye level and at arms length. The cast prevented the two-handed posture that I prefer, but we all have to make do from time to time.

Small-time hoodlums suffer from the same misconceptions as do most of the rest of us. What they see on television and in movies they identify with and treat as reality. They have very little or no personal experience with which to relate, so the directed, acted and edited scene becomes the real world to them, at least in the context of that situation in which they find themselves foreigners. What they always fail to realize is that the real world is very different from the one depicted in those movies and television shows. From the way Moore was handling the girl I could see that he evidently suffered from this delusion.

Real, live, experienced thugs and gunmen know the difference between actions aimed primarily at creating a dramatic effect and acts aimed at keeping themselves alive. Moore had surely seen the hostage situation a hundred times in drama, but had probably never actually been in one himself, up until now. He probably didn't realize that, even in his stooped posture, the girl only shielded about a third of his body. He probably didn't realize that he would never be able to react to the sight or sound of my gun going off in time to shoot the girl, nor did he realize that, even if an involuntary reaction of his finger pulled the trigger, the angle of his gun would produce no more than a flesh wound and powder burns. He also probably hadn't calculated my proximity to him and his hostage. I stood less than forty feet away, watching him down the slightly wavering barrel of my gun, noticing the beads of sweat form on his forehead and upperlip, able to see them run down his chin and neck. He probably didn't realize how much he was gambling on the chance that I wouldn't shoot, or would shoot and miss. I didn't like his odds.

My heart was pounding and I felt light-headed. I was sure I had lost quite a bit of blood by now. I was running out of time before Moore assessed his precarious situation and made the necessary adjustments or, alternatively, I passed out. I kept seeing an image in my head of a set of brass scales, the ones from Nikki's antique shop, tipping wildly back and forth between the relative danger to the girl and myself resulting from the choices I had to make in the next few seconds.

I heard the girl scream as Moore lifted her off the floor by her hair. My arm shifted slightly to the right, following his movement. I squinted the scene into focus as he spun the girl away from his body with his left hand and pivoted the gun to where the barrel pointed into her abdomen. His legs were braced to run, his knees shaking. He was panicking. I knew he intended to shoot her and make a break for it.

I squeezed the trigger, the gun jumped and roared, I heard another scream and saw a huge chunk of Moore's bloody scalp glance off the door frame, all in a split second. As I fell forward into darkness I could hear the girl crying hysterically. I groped my way toward the sound, and as I knelt in front of her my vision returned.

She lay on her back, bottom between his legs, pinned against his stomach and chest by an arm the size of a small tree. His body leaned against the door frame, legs spread wide. The hand on the end of the arm across the girl still held the gun and made small involuntary movements, not quite twitches. The wall, the floor, Moore's body and the girl's hair and clothes were spattered and soaked with varying amounts of blood. I knew I had to get her away from that grisly scene as quickly as possible. I kicked Moore aside and snatched the small body up under my good arm. She writhed and kicked and cried, but I managed to hold on as I stumbled back toward the stairs. I wanted to get to that phone at the downstairs station where I hoped and prayed Plaid Shirt still lay motionless. I fought off the bright pressure of unconsciousness that danced and played around the edges of my vision as I descended the stairs. I don't remember seeing Plaid Shirt, but he didn't bother me. My finger seemed to be taped loosely onto the end of a twelve foot pole made of rubber, and it took me several tries to dial 9-1-1. As soon as I was sure I'd gotten a dispatcher and said "police" with what little voice I could muster, I slid into the corner behind the table, the now whimpering child still clutched against me. The bright edges of the scene before me turned dark and closed in until my vision was just a tiny dot of light in a sea of darkness. I'd just close my eyes and take a nap. Sara was napping. We'd rest here together and everything would be better when we woke up.

14

The phone call brought the police and the press. The night-beat reporters listen to police-band scanners for radio calls just like this one. All I can recall is that it was an absolute circus until a lieutenant-detective was smart enough to try to get the girl and me out of there. She was over the hysterics and into a sort of quiet shock, and she would not let go of me. Any port in a storm, I suppose. To tell the truth, I was reluctant to let go of her. It seemed like I'd gone to an awful lot of trouble to get hold of her in the first place. Besides, I was scared, too.

Consciousness had been returning slowly ever since a uniformed officer with gold-rimmed aviator glasses had appeared in my dream and then stayed on as reality. He was working the girl away from me while the paramedics patched me up temporarily. He started firing questions at me. I tried to answer the questions, but none of them made sense. I really wanted to help.

I kept slipping back into the dream. The cop in the aviator glasses would go into slow motion and begin doing scenes from TV cop shows. He was Dan August, rolling over the hood of a car and coming up with his gun aimed with both hands at the camera. Pow. Then he was David Soul. Where was Starsky? Hell, I'd take either one at this point.

Despite all that I've seen, I've never outgrown my hero worship of cops. In my mind they are the white knights, the calvary, the good guys. Most of my adolescent and young adult life I aspired to become one of those heroes. But I'd washed out, taken a different road and now I spent much of my time on the other side of the coin. Of course, some of my aspirations did come true. I got to carry a gun, go running and jumping around saving damsels in distress, getting the drop on bad guys and I even got to yell "Hold it right there" every once in a while. The reality, however, paled in comparison to my idealized fantasies. Most of the time I got hurt doing the stunts. The bad guys always made me sad rather than angry. I seldom felt righteous indignation that spurred me into flashy action. More often I felt panic or terror that compelled me unsteadily along as I stumbled from one dirty situation to another. The good guys didn't wear white hats. They didn't wear hats at all. They were balding and fat and looked at me like I was an irreverent idiot. They had coffee stains on their ties and they worked in banks or bars or the major appliance department at Montgomery Wards. They wore cheap suits and blue jeans and had ordinary wives and lives. They were not the Lone Ranger or Elliot Ness. They were the you's and the me's. They were all chanting and laughing at me because I couldn't roll across the car like Dan Tanna. Or was it Dan August? They were taunting and prodding me. I retreated in embarrassed silence. I had wet the bed. David Soul stepped forward from the group and leaned over me. He removed his aviator glasses and shook his head sadly. The Judge banged his gavel and pronounced sentence. "You haven't paid your dues, boy. You haven't paid your dues." I cowered in the corner, I did not want to come out from behind the couch.

There are rancid memories from my childhood that come screaming up at me out of some dark pit in my psyche at very disturbing times. Traumatic events seem to summon them, triggering a bizarre and uncontrollable show inside my head. The volume is always at full blast. In the midst of my busy dash between reality and unconsciousness, one of these memories grabbed me and held me down while it gnawed at me. I didn't even struggle to get away. I knew it had me.

The side of my face was pressed against a cold tile floor. Bright red blood spread out on the white tile inches from my eyes. My head hurt and I couldn't seem to move. A shadow above me, out of my field of vision, moved back and forth between the sound of running water and the back of my head. A female voice came from the shadow in the form of muffled sobs and short mumbled phrases. My vision went dark, even though I knew I was holding my eyelids open, and a big man came rushing out of the blackness toward me. He had no face, only the illusion of hair and teeth where a face should be, and blackness when I looked directly at it. His voice came from nowhere and everywhere, it surrounded me and came from within me, howling and cursing and choking on its own words. I could not understand all of the words used, but their profanity was clear. There was a sinister and murderous quality about the man's image, and his arms made threatening gestures toward me. Other objects flew out of the darkness at me; a heavy silver wristwatch, a broken beer bottle, a woman's bra and panties, toy trains and fire engines. The objects all shattered and exploded somewhere behind me. The howling went on and on and it seemed to be amplified by a droning hum and chant of voices in the background. I struggled to raise my hands to cover my ears in an effort to deaden the ungodly din, but my arms would not move. My entire body felt wet and numb, and had the prickly sensation of a limb gone useless due to lack of blood flow. I felt suspended, propelled, torn by the force of the noise. It had the power of a heavy, driving wind. The man tore his T-shirt at the neck, ripping it down across his chest. He wiped his hands again and again on the sides and sleeves of the white shirt, leaving stains of varying color with each wipe. He slapped me and spat at me and then faded into the darkness. My eyes seemed to open and respond to the light, but the noise would not go away. The shadow continued to work overhead, and I could see the front portion of a woman's foot near my face. Cool water ran down my cheeks and neck and diluted the blood on the floor in front of me. I tried to speak and, gagging, was racked with a cough that shook my whole body. The tile floor opened up and I slipped into the dark void that appeared before me. Above the din, as I fell down into the darkness, I could hear the woman crying. A rush of ice-cold air chilled me. There was nothing but noise and blackness. Hands grabbed at me. Sharp sticks prodded at me. I wanted desperately to leave this place. As suddenly as it had leapt upon me, the visceral beast let me up and, brushing me one last time with its hot, foul breath, went away into the blackness. I swam up from the depth of my dream-within-a-dream and gulped down buckets of air. My head still hurt.

Mike Ahearn slipped into the dream, waving his badge around and asking me questions that I didn't know the answers to. Couldn't pass the sergeant's exam, huh? Ahearn rolled across the car. Pow. He led a cheer and then ran for a touchdown through the mud and rain. He put his hands in my pockets and told me not to worry. Then he put on David Soul's glasses and became the cop who had awakened me. I wished they'd make up their minds.

My head rattled back and forth on the stretcher as they wheeled me across the loading dock toward the open ambulance doors. I tried to sit up, but there was someone with his hand on my chest, holding me down. The sky was very black and the red strobes from the police cars and ambulances played off the sides of the surrounding warehouses. I could hear Sara crying, and the sound got closer as we bumped and jangled into the ambulance. I was aware of the movement and the siren as we sped away. Sara had latched on to my good arm. She held it while a paramedic held her. Support group.

The entire left side of my body had become one big blood clot. When we got to the hospital, a nurse was finally able to coax the girl away from me while the doctor worked on my side. It hurt like hell, but it turned out that the knife had done little serious damage, thanks in part to my leather jacket. I suffered mostly from the blood loss and resulting shock.

The detectives that accompanied me to the hospital were very testy. Granted, I had probably loused up their evening by shooting somebody on their shift, but I would have been willing to bet that they didn't feel as lousy as I did. I begged the doctor in emergency to admit me overnight, for observation or whatever, but he seemed to ignore all my not-so-subtle hints while pumping me full of fresh blood and sewing and dressing the wound. I tried to make them all understand that I really wasn't ready to leave the hospital. I had been there less than two hours. I'd hardly gotten my money's worth. Goddamn insurance companies have them throwing people out on the street unless they're tied to a heart-lung machine. Keep those hospital care costs down. The two detectives that were there with me were rather insistent that I accompany them unless it was absolutely, positively, medically necessary that I remain in the hospital. The doctor recognized the tune and knew the step. My two partners and my physician danced around for forty-five minutes before I was finally admitted and wheeled up to a cool, dark room.

Two hours later, my head was throbbing, my mouth was incessantly dry, I was more than a little bit nauseous and the left side of my body, from mid-thigh to neck, ached a dull ache and was annoyed by all the bandages, casts and bindings. The pain shot the doctor had given me worked, but made my head swim up among the fluorescent light fixtures in the ceiling of my hospital room. The nurses were blurry visages in white uniforms. I was as cooperative a suspect as I could be, given my condition. I gave the detectives my gun permit numbers, my investigator's license, date of birth and name of my first and only born. I was finally let off the hook when a medical resident in a Goodwill suit, horn-rimmed glasses and a dirty lab coat became very adamant that I be left alone to rest. The detectives grudgingly conceded, insisting that they be allowed to post a uniformed officer outside my door. The resident didn't like it, but gave in. Nobody asked for my input.

By 3:00 the following afternoon, I had been awakened, questioned, prodded, examined, ignored and dismissed. A nurse was putting a fresh dressing on my wound while two uniformed cops gathered my things into a brown plastic sack. They had been sent to escort me down to headquarters as soon as I was mobile. As I sat on the edge of the bed wincing and withdrawing each time the nurse shifted the bandage, I thought that "mobile" was probably beyond my capabilities at that point. I wore a hospital gown over my blood-stained jeans and rode stiffly in a wheelchair with the two cops flanking me as we departed, and the halls cleared before us like the Red Sea parting for Moses.

The ride downtown was silent and painful. I hadn't been car sick since I was about seven years old, but I came close on that ride.

My reception at Police Headquarters was much better than I expected. Someone there had gotten in touch with Detective Hulmer in Wichita, and he had evidently told the K.C. group that I was a real pain, goddamned independent and apt to skirt the legal technicalities, but that my story would be straight. The fact that Plaid Shirt, from his soft, clean hospital bed, had verified all of my information and acknowledged that they were armed and holding the girl hostage with orders to kill to maintain possession probably didn't hurt my cause either. I did, however, have a lot of questions to answer about why I didn't report the kidnapping. I think they went ahead and interrogated me at the station just to make their point with me on that one. Point made, noted, acknowledged and remembered.

From what I had been able to pick up during the questioning and discussions, it sounded like they were going to have enough solid evidence to tie Freeman in with the kidnapping. Plaid Shirt was talking his heart out. Making that connection gave rise to the logical conclusion that Freeman's operation had been tied in with the drug smuggling. That conclusion, however, was purely circumstantial since they still could not find the drugs, and without that evidence, there was no crime, at least in theory and the minds of District Attorneys. On the other hand, they had plenty of reason to completely unravel all of Freeman's operations, and my guess was that they would find plenty of things during that investigation to hang on him. Looking into someone like Freeman is a little like emptying a cesspool. The deeper you dig the more it stinks.

A policewoman had taken custody of the little girl at the hospital and had stayed with her somewhere in the police facilities during the night. Upon my polite request, they presented Sara for my inspection. She looked a little the worse for wear. She probably thought the same of me.

The police finished their questioning and released me on my own recognizance with a surprising lack of hassle and red tape. Someone else must have put in the good word for me. Surely the phone call to Hulmer hadn't been that impressive. I was so sore and sick that it took total effort and concentration just to sign for my possessions. I was pleased by the fact that they had retrieved my newly-reconstructed jacket from the scene. They had also picked up my gun, performed all of the necessary ballistics testing and were ready to turn it back over to me. The shoulder holster rig, however, had been lost in the shuffle, probably at the hospital. I checked the clip and stuck the Browning in the waistband of my jeans, at the small of my back under my shirt. It was uncomfortable, but I left it there until I had gone down to the garage and claimed my car with a stamped voucher they had given me at the desk. I stuck the gun under the seat, readjusted the rear-view mirror and took off. Driving was sheer terror.

They had notified Linda Matasseren at the number I gave them that her daughter was in their custody. She had requested and authorized them to release the girl to me so that I could bring her back to Wichita, but they had insisted on transporting her themselves, by special dispatch. I can't say I wasn't relieved. It was taking nearly everything I had just to transport myself. I drove, very slowly, back to the Ramada to retrieve my belongings and check myself out.

As beat up and bone weary as I was, I could sense that something was wrong as soon as I pushed the door to my room open. The dark cubicle held the air of violation that can mean anything from the maid having been there to a person lurking behind the door. I moved quickly to a position where I could check all of the possible hiding places, leaving the door to the outside walkway open. My hand found its way to the pistol grip in the back waistband of my pants, returned there when I'd exited the car downstairs. I slid back the action and worked a round up into the chamber, holding the gun against my thigh as I clicked the safety off. No sense waving it around and giving some maid heart failure as she came out of the bathroom.

A quick but cautious check revealed that I was the only living thing in the room. I dropped my gun on the bed and shut the door. As I turned and faced back into the room, I realized what had caught my subconscious attention. My blue gym bag sat in the chair opposite the foot of the bed. I had left it on the bed the previous day after outfitting myself for my assault on the warehouse. I was sure. I specifically remembered leaning over the bed and zipping it up. I picked up the bag and sorted carefully through its contents. Nothing was missing. It was hard to tell if other things in the room had been disturbed, but the two or three items of clothing I'd thrown onto hangers in the open closet next to the bathroom had definitely been searched. The hangers were evenly spaced and the clothes relatively straight on the hangers. That is not the way I hang things up. I start at one end, throw the clothes haphazardly onto the hangers, and shove them in a bunch together as I move on to the next item. Some other hand had touched the jackets, shirt and pants that hung before me. Maids don't usually straighten your clothes. It occurred to me that any halfway competent television detective would have slipped a matchstick or piece of paper into the door and left the "do not disturb" sign on the outside doorknob so that there would have been some definite sign that someone had invaded the room. When it came right down to it, though, not only had nothing been taken, there was nothing there that mattered to anyone. My gut told me that someone had been in my room for purposes other than to clean and pick up after me. That was sufficient to shoot a cold chill along my spine. Just one more anxiety to add to what I considered more than my full share. I was in great shape.

When I had finished my inspection, I phoned Linda Matasseren. I told her that they would not be letting me bring Sara home, but that she would probably arrive before I did. I had asked that they deliver her to my house, and I instructed Linda to wait there for her and for me.

"The cop that called said you'd been hurt," Linda said, with what I thought for a moment was a note of concern. "I'm not responsible for medical expenses, am I?" The note of concern turned sour.

"I wasn't hurt too badly," I grunted. "I'm walking around, and no, you won't be responsible. I've got insurance that will cover all the medical." I didn't bother her with any of the details. I doubt she was interested.

"Where did you find her?" she asked.

"At a warehouse here, a shipping point for an outfit called Continental Sporting Goods."

"Oh," was her reply.

"They didn't find the drugs, in case you're wondering. A guy named Freeman told me that he'd already located them, but the last report I got, which was hard to get at all, and almost twenty-four hours old, was that the police had taken every inch of the warehouse and all of Freeman's company offices apart, but there was nothing like what everyone's been looking for. I guess your husband's got it pretty well tucked away. Or maybe Freeman does, who knows?"

"I don't care anymore," she said. I was sure all she really cared about at this point was getting the girl back. She thanked me again without much warmth and hung up. I sat on the bed feeling empty. I'd probably been a little short with her. She had a right to ask about the financial aspects, after all, she was paying. Come on, Case, what were you expecting, brass bands and pledges of eternal gratitude and loyalty? After all, you were just doing your job. It's what the lady was paying you for. I pouted, nonetheless. She didn't even offer to get the blood stains out of my cape and tights.

Then I called Janette. She was home and feeling well enough to want to get to the office in the morning. I knew I could count on Mark to keep her in check.

As I was starting to pack, there was a knock at my door. It was Penny. I was so relieved to see her standing there in her ugly brown uniform that I almost screamed. I did a few internal cartwheels in response to the release of suppressed fear, doing my best to hide the evidence in my eyes.

"You've been avoiding me," I said, carefully waiting for a response. To hell with being coy and indirect.

"That's my line," she said with a tight smile. "Lisa Brown called yesterday morning and wanted to change shifts with me. I was beat anyway, so I said fine. I took her shift and finished up at two o'clock this morning. I came by your room, but you weren't here. Lisa was supposed to leave a message for you before she went off shift."

"I was involved elsewhere," I said, rubbing the back of my neck. "The message could very well be downstairs, I haven't been by the desk." I could feel a rush of excitement and relief at finding out that she had not been purposely avoiding seeing me. At the same time, I was thanking the heavens and whatever powers that be for her safety and well-being. I had been given absolution for my stupidity.

"Involved elsewhere?" she said sarcastically, shaking her head. "Case, you made the papers and the prime time news. Was it all true?"

"I don't know," I said, surprised. "I haven't seen a paper or a newscast. I can tell you from my point of view that I'm not feeling like much of a human being this morning."

"They were practically calling you a hero."

"Distortion of the facts by the press."

She looked at me long and hard in the heavy silence. I looked back. A little furrow formed in her forehead, right between the dark eyebrows. I was sitting on the bed and she in the chair. She finally stood up and walked the two steps it took to stand directly in front of me. She looked steadily into my eyes, our gazes locked. I felt myself starting to melt. I would later often recall the sight of those lovely eyes at that very moment, as they made their unwavering mark on me.

"You can be my hero anytime," she said breathlessly, putting her arms around me. It was corny, but I didn't care. It was what I needed to hear. I pulled her close, wrapping my good arm around her buttocks and burying the side of my head into her abdomen. She stroked my hair softly with one hand and rested the other lightly on the back of my neck. I stood and we kissed. Not a long, passionate kiss, but one of familiarity and comfort. You could never have convinced me at that moment that I had known this woman for only two days.

"I'm only on a break," she whispered hoarsely. "I knew you'd be leaving, and I wanted to make sure I had a chance to say goodbye." She looked up at me with a pained expression. "I've got to get back." She leaned up and we kissed again, softly.

"Call me sometime," she said at the door.

"I'm not very good at that," I admitted. "I'll write, though."

"Write me, I'd like that," she said. She pulled a pen and paper out of her purse and scribbled down an address. I got one of my cards out of my billfold and gave it to her.

"By the way," I said, "I'm sorry I missed you last night."

"Me too," She said with an ornery grin as she opened the door.

"I wish I could stay and mend for a couple of days, but I've got some business to take care of."

"I know," she said, turning as she stepped out the door. "Bye."

I wandered about the room and thought sweet thoughts for a few minutes after she left before I finished my packing and got ready to check out. I was finding that the simplest of tasks—walking, packing, moving—were pure and total effort. I was bandaged, stitched, plastered and taped from hip to shoulder on the left side of my body, and the various areas of injury ached and burned beneath the medicinal bindings. Muscles and joints smarted and complained at any exertion of pressure or movement. Plaid Shirt had really put me through the paces, and Moore had caused me to inflict a few bruises and cuts on myself while I was avoiding his bullets. I found myself snickering at the fact that, despite a gnawing guilt over Moore's death, I felt absolutely no remorse over having put ol' Plaid Shirt in the hospital. I hoped he hated the food.

The stairs outside my room were hell on my knees as I carried my stuff to the car. I checked the shotgun when I loaded my bag into the trunk. It was still there, but it had been moved. The K.C. police were very thorough. It was a quiet little piece of heaven to pour myself into the car and sit with the motor running for a few minutes.

15

It was a long, empty drive back to Wichita. I seemed to be swinging like a pendulum from one extreme of emotion to another, a manic depressive at the wheel of a green Chevy on I-35 in the midst of the Flint Hills. By the time I reached the halfway point, I was feeling about as low as I could ever recall feeling. I couldn't put a finger on the source of the depression, but I was fairly certain it centered around the emotions and feelings I was having about having to kill Moore. I had shot at, and hit, several people in the course of my various endeavors, but Moore was the first one I had solely and directly been responsible for killing. The death had been so graphic and unquestionable that I had never enjoyed the fleeting suspicion that he would live. He had died instantaneously at the will and direction of my hand.

I often curse myself for being generally heartless and unfeeling. I have the ability to pull myself away from a situation, even one of intense personal feeling and intimacy, and view it with a very cold, logical eye. What kind of a person can observe and analyze the ones he loves like a clinician, carefully noting apparent motives and motivations, second-guessing intentions and coldly classifying behavior? Such an animal as me, self-styled behaviorist, believing that there is a reason for every action, a meaning behind every utterance. Me, the hard, unfeeling stone man, who carries off the charade of true human emotion for everyone's benefit but his own.

And then there are times when I get lumpy and teary over some stupid goddamn movie, or the Fourth-of-July celebration at the Statue of Liberty. Perhaps it is at those moments that the pent-up emotions and vulnerabilities from all the closer more threatening situations come to the surface, at a time when no one can share them or penetrate my defenses. At a time when I'm safe.

I rolled through thoughts of my cold nature and the reaction I was having to Moore's death as I drove. I could remember the evening when Annie and I had finally agreed that a divorce was not only imminent, but necessary. That was the last time I could remember this kind of pain, but I had felt less grief for our marriage than I felt now for Moore. Or maybe it was the displacement theory all over again. Remorse over the death of something relatively impersonal to compensate for the suppressed anguish over the death of something so close and so dear that to express it would be a total compromise of spirit. What kind of son-of-a-bitch lives that way? It was a form of existence lower than dirt. There was a coarseness on the inside of my soul that it hurt to touch, so I left it alone rather than to try to smooth it out.

At one point during the drive, I got to thinking about AIDS. Ironically enough, it wasn't Penny I was worried about. My concern was over the blood they'd pumped into my thirsty veins at the hospital. I didn't know how much they'd given me, but I knew that a lot had leaked out. The media blitz on the subject had everyone more than a little antsy about any potential way of contracting the disease, and I wondered about the screening policies at the K.C. hospital where I'd been.

Suddenly, I laughed out loud at myself. Here I was worrying about the outside chance of contracting Acquired Immune Deficiency Syndrome from a blood transfusion. Me, the guy who'd been attacked with lethal lumber, stabbed in a knife fight and shot at in the darkness from nearly pointblank range by a semi-professional thug, all in the span of the last five days. I couldn't help but see it as funny. Like I'd told Penny, danger is a relative thing.

When I got home, it was after 9:30 and there were two cars parked out front, both unmistakably unmarked police vehicles. One had Missouri plates, the other was City of Wichita. As I pulled in the drive, two faintly familiar cop-types got out of the Missouri car. I could see the girl lying down in the back seat. Hulmer and his partner emerged from the Wichita car.

It seemed that Linda had not been there when the K.C. police had shown up with her daughter, about an hour ago. They called Hulmer in because of the assurances he'd given them over the phone to help cut me loose. We all went inside. I phoned Linda's house. No answer. I phoned Janette's. Mark answered the phone on the first ring.

"She's sleeping, Case," he said.

"I'm looking for Linda," I told him.

"We haven't seen her."

The two K.C. cops didn't want to leave the girl with me. Nothing I said could convince them.

After what seemed like an eternity, Hulmer came to the rescue. "If the lad says he's authorized to take custody of the girl, then he is," Hulmer finally interjected. "No shit. Believe him."

They took his word reluctantly and went on their way. Hulmer sent Hart, his partner, to the car and gave me a stern song-and-dance about using good judgement and not being such a jackass. I nodded a lot and respectfully showed him the door. He was still lecturing as he went down the front steps.

Sara had not awakened, even when they brought her in from the car, so I put her down in the guest bed. While I was in the room, I checked through Linda's things. All the bags she had come with were still there, but her purse was gone. That made me feel a little better. When you leave by means other than of your own volition, you don't often get to take your purse. I closed the door behind me as Sara settled into the bedding, thumb in mouth. I went into my bedroom and picked up the Browning Automatic, which I'd carried in from the car and left on the dresser. It felt strangely light in my hand and cold to my touch. This was it. This was the machine that had enabled me to snuff out the life of another human being from far enough away to avoid the splattering blood. Sara had not been so lucky. I felt a slow surge move through my back and gut and head. I pulled the clip out of the gun, removed the remaining rounds, and laid the parts together neatly in the bottom of my dresser drawer. The ammunition went in an otherwise empty gun case under the bed. I stopped with the drawer only halfway shut, opened it back up and removed the gun. I fished an old shoebox off of the top shelf of my closet, re-wrapped the Browning in its rag, put it in the box and pushed the box to the back corner of the closet, behind a bunch of shoes and an old wastebasket. I had a feeling that it would stay there for quite a while. I closed the closet doors, dropped the bullets into the gun case and washed my hands in the bathroom sink. Gun oil is messy.

I had been fretting and stewing and pacing around the house for about an hour when the phone rang.

"You seen your client?" Hulmer asked in a very open-ended way.

"Not since you were here," I told him.

"Uh-huh," came the tired-sounding response on the other end of the line. "Well, you'd better know that we finally connected up your friends in Kansas City with an outfit called Continental Commercial Laundry here in town. We sent some boys 'round to check them out and found two people had been shot just a few minutes earlier. One was dead. The other's not in very good shape, but he did manage to tell us that 'Linda got the stuff'. I'd say there's a fair chance that this involves your client somehow, wouldn't you, kid?"

I dropped the phone, ran into the bedroom and went ripping through the dresser drawer where I keep my hand-guns. For all the ritual I had undergone with the 9mm Browning, I hadn't even checked on my other two weapons, a .38 Police Special and a .357 Magnum. They were both gone. Damn. Hulmer told me not to leave, and reminded me that if I failed to detain Linda in the event she showed up, I would be an accessory to the shootings. I told him testily that I knew the law. I was tired and cranky.

I thought about what would happen when Linda returned for her daughter. I was sure of what I had to do. I didn't like it much. But any options that I might have had were eliminated by the arrival of Hulmer and Hart in an unmarked car. They parked themselves in my living room. Sara woke up and asked for her mommy. I told her she was on her way. I fed her, she played for a little while with the toys I keep in the guest closet for Jenny and went back to bed. No Linda.

Hulmer and Hart eventually left, letting me know there would be someone watching the house. I didn't think it was a threat or warning, but Hulmer seemed somewhat disappointed to find me in this situation. So was I.

I was also very relieved to have been lucky enough to find Sara before Freeman decided to dispose of her. There was no doubt in my mind that having recovered the drugs on his own, he would have eventually killed her. You count your blessings, I guess.

16

The best picture that the Police were later able to piece together was this:

Linda had known enough about the people involved in the drug operation to recognize the names "Continental" or "Freeman," or both, when I mentioned them over the phone. Continental's main laundry facility was located in Wichita and was also owned by Freeman. It was a natural spin-off business. They serviced mostly sports and athletic programs throughout the area, a service easily sold right along with the sports equipment and specialized enough to require their particular services. They had evidently seen the regular and far-reaching routes and travels of the laundry business as the best system for distribution of the finally processed coke. Or maybe they just wanted it in Wichita rather than Kansas City. In any event, Linda put her own two-and-two together and, with the help of a thus-far unidentified male, took the stash from the Continental Laundry facility, where it had evidently been held since Freeman laid his hands on it. The plant was shut down for the evening, and Linda and her accomplice broke in through a basement window. The drugs had been removed from the shipping containers and stored in a back office area. There were two guys posted to keep an eye on the loot. Linda and her friend had cased the inside of the plant and snooped around for over an hour before they jumped the two guards and shot them. One died and one was paralyzed from the waist down with a shot that caught him at the base of his spine while he was trying to get away. Linda and her accomplice loaded the boxes containing the drugs out a window that opened onto an alley behind the building into what a witness thought was a bronze-colored van. That was the last anyone had seen of them.

The police insisted that I keep Sara at my house for five or six days, with the idea of using her as bait. Although I had come to the conclusion that it was pointless, I was in no position to argue with them about it. I knew by then that Linda Matasseren did not intend to return for the child. She had turned out to be a user, and a very good one. She had left me feeling violated and victimized, a feeling I have had to deal with rarely in my life. Although I'm one of the first to rise to the losing cause or hopeless crusade, I always do so with a cynical knowledge of the reality of the situation. I try never to kid myself. But this time someone had kidded me, conned me, pulled the wool over my eyes, used me. It made me feel stupid, gullible and very angry. Particularly since the real victim was a helpless child.

At 9:30 on the morning of the third day, I was awakened by my doorbell. I had been sleeping late every morning, since I had no real desire to go in to the office and address the chaos that had surely set in with Janette on temporary leave. Besides, the police wanted me to stick around as much as possible in case Linda tried to make contact, and they weren't exactly helping me out with the babysitting for Sara. I was on my own as far as she was concerned. I had been staying home or taking Sara with me for the most part, but I had to rely on Megan Ritter a couple of times. Megan is the fourteen-year-old that lives down the block and takes care of Jenny when she's staying with me and I need some help. She's a sweet kid, good with little girls, mature for her age, reliable and works for two bucks an hour. I considered asking Hulmer for reimbursement on the fourteen dollar tab I racked up with Megan during the week, and then thought better of it. No sense pushing my luck.

Sara was still asleep when, bleary-eyed, I pulled on an old pair of grey sweats and answered the door. I was confronted with two guys in suits and raincoats who I assumed were associates of the local detective division checking in on me. I squinted at them myopically. They looked like blurry detectives. One of them smelled of pipe smoke.

"Yeah?" I muttered disdainfully.

"Mr. Freeman sent us to have a word with you," the one on the left said. He was slightly taller than the other, and had dark brown or black hair, I couldn't quite tell. His companion's hair seemed lighter and he wore glasses. You don't get much more detail than that when you're as nearsighted as I am, even from only five or six feet away. The mention of Freeman's name had given me a start. I was sure it showed

"Come on in," I said, cautiously stepping back and opening the door. I rubbed my hand across my face and glanced out beyond my guests for a sign of any sort that the police were on the scene. I couldn't see that far.

"Have a seat in there," I said, motioning toward the living room. "I'll be right back." They didn't object to my departure into the bedroom to get my glasses. I had no time for contacts, these guys would have to take me as I was. I could tell by the foot sounds on the tile entryway that at least one of them was hanging back to listen for traces of a phone conversation or the telltale noise of a weapon. I grabbed my glasses and hurried back. No need to arouse suspicion.

I was reasonably sure that they weren't there to do me harm. Coming to the front door in broad daylight is not exactly the safest way to bump someone off or rough them up. Besides, these two did not look like muscle. They looked more like they were from the Executive Office. I kept trying to sneak glances out the window, just the same.

"We're not here to beat around the bush," the one with the dark hair said. He seemed to be the spokesman. "Mr. Freeman wants the Matasseren woman. He's willing to retain you at a very attractive rate to represent him in the, ah, location. That would, of course, be premised on the fact that you were no longer employed by Mrs. Matasseren and would have no

conflict of interest or problem of client confidentiality." This
guy was good. It didn't sound like a buy-off.

I studied the two while Dark Hair made his pointed pitch.
He was seated on the couch, directly in front of the chair I
had chosen. His pal was at the other end of the couch, one
hip hiked up onto the arm where it curved into the back.
Both had kept their overcoats on. I could tell from what I
could see of their outfits; pantlegs, collars, shoes and ties;
that they were tastefully but not expensively dressed. I had to
assume that they both wore guns under their coats. Glasses
had noticed me looking out the window, and was keeping his
own watch on the outside.

"I'm afraid I can't help you guys," I said, looking at Dark
Hair. I settled back into the chair and hooked one leg up over
the arm. My bare toes pressed against the cold wall. "As a
matter of fact, I'm sitting here right now as a decoy for the
police in the hope that Linda will contact me. Her little girl,
the actual bait in this operation, is asleep right now in the
other room. You remember Sara, I had to take her away from
you guys. Some shit must have really hit the fan over that
one." My voice had taken on a little edge.

"We don't know anything about that," Dark Hair said. "We
were sent down here strictly to establish a working relationship with you in locating Mrs. Matasseren." Glasses lifted
himself from his perch and strolled over to the picture window, standing off to one side. I couldn't tell whether he had
seen something or not.

"I hope you understand," Dark Hair went on, "that Mr.
Freeman has instructed us to obtain your services or secure
your cooperation at whatever price or in whatever manner is
necessary." I wasn't sure if I was supposed to be salivating or
trembling. I wasn't doing either, but I was feeling a little
anxious.

Glasses caught my eye as he turned around, and I saw a
startled look on his face when he glanced up. "Larry," he said
quietly, looking at Dark Hair and motioning with his chin

toward the dining room area. Dark Hair, who I think we had now determined was named Larry, turned around on the couch to look over his left shoulder into the dining room at about the same time that I shifted my gaze to follow Glasses' direction. We both saw Detective Hulmer standing there simultaneously. Hulmer was leaning against the doorway into the kitchen with his arms crossed over his torso and one foot propped up against the opposite doorjamb. I could see the top part of his service revolver in his right hand, just behind the inside of his left elbow.

"Go on, Gents," he said, "it was just getting interestin'." He grinned a grin that was neither pleasant nor amused. It simply crossed his face and then went away. Larry and Glasses were staring at him. I realized that I was smirking, and struggled to suppress it. Hulmer must have come in through the kitchen door while we were having our little chat. Although I had been facing the spot where he stood almost directly, I had not noticed when he had taken up his position in the doorway. He very well could have been there the whole time.

"I'm not here to give you boys any trouble," Hulmer said in a very matter-of-fact tone. "In case you're interested, I'm Lieutenant-Detective Thomas J. Hulmer of the Wichita Police Department, and I can verify Mr. Casey's story here that he knows nothing of the whereabouts of our suspect, Linda Matasseren. He is indeed cooperating with us in an effort to bring the suspect in, but we've had no luck so far. You might say that Mr. Casey is otherwise occupied at the moment, and that he's unable to accept your kind and generous offer. In fact, right this very minute you two assholes are probably blowing the whole thing just by being here. I'd suggest that you report back to your boss-man that no one down here's interested in his propositions, and that he'd better stay the hell out of my way."

As if he were responding to some sort of cue, Larry stood up abruptly and looked at Glasses. Larry had been able to maintain his composure, but Glasses looked as if his tail were tucked between his legs. Both of them moved swiftly to the front door and exited quietly. I didn't see them out. About thirty seconds later, we heard a car start from about two houses down the block and then drive off. Hulmer and I stared at each other in silence until after the sound of the car had faded. Hulmer unfolded his arms, tucked his gun underneath his left arm and stood away from the door frame.

"Watch yer ass," he said, pointing his finger at me. He turned and walked through the kitchen and out the back door. Thank heaven for the cavalry.

I went to see Paul Matasseren in the county Jail later that same day. The police had arranged things with the District Attorney's office so that he was being held under an absolutely stifling bond. He didn't seem to be complaining or trying to do anything about it. He probably felt like he was safer on the inside. He probably was. He had heard about Linda's big heist, and to say that he wasn't pleased would be an understatement. There's a much faster and more accurate line of communication within a prison structure than the omnipotent media could ever hope to create out in the free world. Paul Matasseren had probably known all the details of how his ex-wife had screwed him before the cops even had the scene roped off.

"That rotten bitch," Matasseren said when I asked about Linda, "Hell, no I don't know where she'd go. She'll keep it that way if she's smart. I'll kill her, or have it done, if I ever get the chance."

I tried to ease into the subject of Sara. His reaction was much the same as it had been about Linda.

"I ain't takin' care of that fuckin' kid," he snarled through clenched teeth. "I never wanted her. It was the only way that bitch could get me to marry her. And don't come serving any support papers on me, sucker. I'll say that the kid's not mine. That bitch screwed around enough, it might not be. Don't

come leanin' on me about that kid." So much for appealing to
his fatherly affections.

After the six days had passed with no result, Hulmer finally
agreed with me that Linda was not coming back. They had
no leads. Janette helped me get Sara set up through the
Social and Rehabilitation Services for temporary custody. I
insisted that they place her in a foster home immediately, and
I personally escorted the social worker and Sara to the first
meeting with the foster parents. All this made me quite un-
popular with the SRS, but I didn't care. I felt responsible for
the child. There was more than that, though. We shared a
common bond. We had both been pawns in a bloody game of
chess, where the fortress to be conquered consisted of a few
hundred bags of white powder. Our lives had been twisted,
used and forever marked by people who were nothing more
than cold machines, programmed to pursue that greatest of
all temptations, the dollar. We were kindred spirits.

The afternoon of the day that I took Sara and the Social
Worker to the foster parent's home, I spotted an innocuous
looking gold sedan going through a red light behind me. I
drove around a little and bought a Coke at McDonalds, just
to make sure it was tailing me. It was. My first thought was of
my previous visitors, the envoys of goodwill from Joe Freeman's organization. I suppose that the logical reaction should
have been fear, but I was feeling a bit put upon and had just
about had it with all the friendly folks who wanted a piece of
my hide, in one form or another, to use as a doormat. My
reaction to the gold sedan was to get pissed off.

I cranked the Chevy into the parking lot of an office building off of Twenty-first Street and pulled around behind the
building into the lot of a restaurant that was situated in the
lower level of the north side. Because of the configuration of
the building and lots, there was only one opening into the
restaurant's lot, right off of the main parking area for the
complex. I pulled into the lot, drove about thirty feet down
along the frontage of Armour's Cafe and Grill and waited.

The gold Ford swung blindly into the lot and, upon seeing my car, turned abruptly down the first row of parking. I slapped the car into reverse and slid quickly back along the curb until I had the opening to the lot completely blocked with the length of the vehicle. The Ford circled aimlessly through the almost empty parking area. I got out of my car and leaned against the driver's door facing toward the lot with my right hand in the pocket of my jeans. My left arm was still in the cast. I slid the hand halfway out of my pocket and back in again. Just checking. I wanted to look casual, but I wanted to be able to move quickly if I needed to. Reassuring to know that the old Levis weren't too tight. I must have been doing a better job of keeping fit than I realized. Levis are usually a pretty good barometer. I peered silently at the Ford, which was now parked along the curb at the opposite side of the lot. I tried to look tough and challenging. I was, as Carole King would say, in the mood for a little confrontation. I was reasonably sure that they wouldn't try to shoot me or run me down right there in full view of the mid-afternoon restaurant patrons. I was also reasonably sure that they wouldn't keep circling around the parking lot until I got bored and left. Either way, there was only one way to find out. I waited.

Just as I was wondering what I would do if someone came out of Armour's and got into their car, the gold Ford pulled away from the far curb and drove directly toward me at a deliberate but not threatening pace. Its occupants must have arrived at a decision. I hugged my right arm against my body and was comforted by the close but not yet familiar bulge of a brand new Smith and Wesson .357 Magnum on my hip under the loose sweatshirt that I wore. As the front end of the Ford Granada slowed and stopped several feet in front of me, I could see that the driver was the same guy that I'd noticed in the Mexican restaurant up in Kansas City. Bingo! I couldn't see the passenger's face behind the lowered sun visor, but I more than expected it to be one of the two guys that had visited me at home. The passenger shifted in the seat, opened the door and slid out. It took a second or two for my brain to shift gears and identify the person coming out of the car, but when I had recovered from the initial surprise I realized that it was Mike Ahearn. He was dressed in brown wool slacks, a tweed jacket under an open grey wool overcoat and a tan knit tie, but it was indeed Michael R. Ahearn. He looked a little uncomfortable. I wondered if it was the clothes or the somewhat embarrassing situation he found himself in.

"Howdy, Case," he said in an apologetic tone.

"Ahearn," I said flatly, nodding. I couldn't come up with anything else to say. My mind was racing, trying to fit the pieces together. Mike shut the car door and walked over to where I stood.

"I told Gibbons back there that you'd spot a tail," he said, motioning toward the figure behind the wheel. "He's K.C. Detectives. We've been assigned together on sort of a co-op effort. You're it."

I squinted at him and tried not to look like I was expending as much effort as I was trying to make sense out of what he was saying. The strain must have showed, because he went on with his explanation.

"After the incident up in Newton, I had to make a report on our conversation. I'm sorry, but I had to. I'd been on that case up until they busted Matasseren, so I had a duty to follow up. After the attack on your secretary and the Matasseren broad they put me on assignment to shadow you. I didn't like it, but they figured I was the best one for the job, so I was stuck with it." He shifted his stance uncomfortably and rubbed his eyes with one hand. "I sort of lost track of you for a couple of days, and found out later you'd been down in Dallas. They've tied that all together now, but we didn't know anything about the Dallas activity at that time. Anyway, when you took off for K.C., they hooked me up with the Department there and gave me to Sergeant Gibbons. We've been on you ever since you checked in at the Ramada."

I looked up at the gray sky and let out a long, slow breath. It was starting to make sense, and some of my denseness was beginning to show.

"Where were you guys when I was in the warehouse?" I asked.

"We were down the alley a couple of blocks. We didn't hear any of the fireworks, I guess we were too far away. Fact is, we didn't know anything was going on 'til we saw the ambulances and squad cars pull up. We didn't even catch a radio call. We got there right as they were getting ready to haul you out. You saw me, but I don't think it registered. I wasn't sure you were going to make it."

"Great," I said, shaking my head. "You guys are there every step of the way until I need you, and then you've got your head up your ass."

"Case," Mike said in a defensive tone, his hand up in a holding gesture, "you were on your own on this thing. You chose to work outside the system, and that means unnecessary risks. We weren't there to give you backup, just to see what you were up to and where you'd lead us. You could have come to us, worked with us. We knew about the girl. We could have helped. I kept telling them you'd come to us with it."

"You knew about Freeman?" I asked. I was wondering how far they had been willing to let me hang out.

"No," he said, looking down at his shoes. "We didn't even connect up Freeman when you went to his office. We ran checks on every business in that office park and came up with nothing that cross-referenced with this case. We couldn't figure out what you were doing in there. We figured it was another one of your little side excursions."

"Jesus," was all I could say. I felt a momentary surge of anger at the remark about my "side excursions," but managed to suppress it. That was an unrelated issue at the moment.

"Case, I don't like this any better than you do. I'm just trying to do my job."

"I suppose you were the ones who went through my room in K.C., too," I said.

"Not us," Mike said quickly. "I can't guarantee that somebody from Gibbons' team didn't do it, but I know we were never in there. From what Hulmer tells me, Freeman's boys have been poking at you some. Could have been them."

"Uh-huh," I said. His explanation didn't satisfy me. "So what are you guys doing still sniffing around my asshole like a couple of horny mutts?"

"Hey pal, don't get snippy with me. They figure you're the only link to Linda Matasseren. They want her bad. They figure you're helping her out, Robin Hood." There was anger in his voice. Now I'd managed to piss him off.

"Give Sergeant Gibbons my regards," I said as I stood away from the car and opened the door. "I'll try to drive slow enough so that you won't be embarrassed by having to tell your superiors that you've lost me again."

"Case," Mike said as I got into the car and shut the door. I didn't hear the rest of what he might have said, I started the engine and drove off.

I fumed as I drove. My feelings were hurt. I was mad. I felt insulted. I was very tired of the whole depressing affair and I was angry. Angry mostly, I realized, at myself. I knew Ahearn had been right in doing what he felt he had to do. I'd been playing both ends against the middle. I could hardly expect favorable treatment. I had probably been lucky to get the breaks they'd given me. I realized that Ahearn's presence must have been what made things go so smoothly with the Kansas City police. Still, the whole thing offended me. I hoped I could get over the resentment I felt toward Ahearn. I didn't have many friends, I could hardly afford to lose one. In the back of my mind, though, I was picking away at a little piece of instinct which was telling me that Ahearn had some real suspicions about my involvement with Linda Matasseren and the situation as a whole. Suspicion breeds contempt, and contempt will quickly rot any relationship, no matter how strong or long-standing it might be. That thought disturbed me a great deal.

The next week, things seemed to fall back into normalcy. I hit the office to clean up all the messes that had been generated in the absence of both Janette and me. Janette was back in the office, unable to stand being at home any longer. The police, both in K.C. and Wichita, finally pumped enough information out of me so that they were willing to leave me alone and out of their respective pending investigations, at least for the time being. I made several visits to Sara's new foster home and was very pleased to find her adjusting better than I could have imagined. Six-year-olds are a lot tougher than most of us adults, or so we like to think. I only hoped that this whole experience would not leave scars that would take years to heal. I hoped that the whole thing would find it's way back into some inaccessible part of little Sara's brain, darkened and irretrievable. I kept seeing two images in my head over and over again when I thought of Sara. One was of her small face, covered with blood and screaming hysterically, trapped beneath Moore's big, dead arm. The other was of the same small face, reacting as the Social Worker and I introduced her to the foster family. Her eyes were dark, silent beacons of fear, disappointment and disbelief. Both images were equally disturbing. Neither would go away no matter how hard I willed them to. I was sure it was worse for Sara.

Janette commented on several occasions that I seemed to be smiling a little more than I had been over the previous few months. I told her that it was an illusion created in her mind, an aftereffect of the concussion. She would smile knowingly and say "umm-hmmm." Penny for your thoughts.

The time and effort I had put into helping little Sara motivated me to spend some more time with my own daughter. Maybe I felt guilty. Maybe I wasn't so different from Linda

Matasseren. Maybe Jenny would someday feel just as abandoned as Sara was.

I spent most of the first Saturday afternoon and evening in December with Ann and Jenny. We went Christmas shopping, out to dinner and rented some Care Bears video tapes to watch at home. Before the second tape was done, I picked a sleeping Jenny up off of the couch and carried her to her room. I tucked her carefully in under the lace-ruffled comforter and gave her a quiet, lingering kiss. Her check was warm and smooth beneath my lips. Her tiny hand clutched the edge of the sheet and her breathing was soft and regular. I was missing a lot of my child's life. This was no way to be a father. "'Night, Doodles," I whispered in the darkness.

When I went back out to the living room Annie had rewound the video tapes, put them back into the shopping bag and was holding it out to me.

"Could you take these back tomorrow?" She asked. I got the feeling I was being dismissed.

After I'd put on my coat, I moved clumsily over to where Annie waited by the front door and embraced her. She clutched her arms together against my chest, but did not resist. She leaned her head against my shoulder in an accepting manner.

"Promise me you'll always tell Jenny how much I love her," I said, my jaw resting on the top of her head. "Promise me you'll never let her think that I'm not around because I don't love her."

"I do and I will," Annie said softly.

"You know I still love you," I said, aware of my chin moving across the top of her head, and down to the side near her ear.

"Not enough," she said gently into my arm, "not enough."

The cold made my eyes sting as I hustled out to my car. Or maybe it was the contact lenses.

17

The week before Christmas, I got two very interesting deliveries in the mail. The first was small and unassuming, but made my heart leap into my throat. It was a plain envelope, no return address, post-marked in Findlay, Ohio. It contained two money orders, purchased from an Illinois Stop N-Shop convenience store, and this handwritten note:

"Dear Mr. Casey,
I'm sure you don't think much of me as a person after what I did. I was never much of a mother to Sara, so she will be better off this way. I know that you will see that she is taken care of, so I'm sending you this money to help take care of her. I will try to send more sometime, but this may have to last a long time. Give her kisses for me.

Linda

P.S. The smaller check is for you. Thank you for everything you did for me. I'm sorry."

Both money orders were made payable to me. The one intended for Sara's use was made out for $20,000. Mine was for $10,000. I closed myself up in my office with my dictation machine and drafted a trust for Sara, with myself and the Kansas State Bank as co-trustees. The money would be invested and used for Sara's health, education and welfare upon written request to me and approval by both co-trustees. Any person having legal custody of Sara could apply until she reached age eighteen, when the requests would come from and be paid directly to her. No one could touch it any other way.

Janette had the instrument finalized by that afternoon and I took it down to the bank to set up the account and arrange details with David Kravens, one of the Trust Officers who I knew there. I was sure that I could count on him to ask very few questions and say very little. I didn't want any of the authorities trying to deny Sara what little bit of help the money might provide on some cockeyed theory of evidence or a claim that it was fruits of a crime. The account balance opened with $28,000. Not much to start a life on, but a little bit of an edge for someone who'd already been set back more than her share. It was a strange and horrible gift to leave a child, a tainted and vile legacy.

The trust had almost opened with the full $30,000, but then greed took over. I had more than earned the fee, but for what result? The death of one man by my own hand? Indirect accessory to a felony killing? Semi-orphaning a six-year-old child? Guilt and a bad taste in my mouth kept creeping up on me when I would try to estimate hours spent and actual expenses. I kept thinking that it wasn't fair, not to Sara. She shouldn't be stuck with any more of her mother's bad judgments. She had already been burdened with enough of those. I compromised on two thousand, enough to cover most of the expenses, some medical (I'd lied about the insurance) and provide a nominal fee for the time involved. So why did I feel shitty about it? I kept teetering back and forth. Life goes on, and I had bills to pay. The lady had sent me ten grand, I was only taking two. But then again, little Sara needed all the help she could get. I was a big boy. I resigned myself to the fact that it was a no-win situation and stuck the two thousand in my office account. Maybe I'd feel better about it tomorrow.

I was probably feeling worse because my hopes had been dashed by Linda's note. Until she sent the money, I had harbored the faint hope that she would return for Sara, send for her, anything. The finality of a $30,000 sacrifice offering by a pagan currency-worshiper was both sickening and heartrending to me. Sara would never again see her mother. Her father, who had no interest in her anyway, would most likely spend the rest of his life in one kind of prison or another. I swallowed back a few tears for Sara. Maybe there were a few salty tears there for myself as well. I felt deep inside that the whole experience had further dirtied my already soiled inner landscape. The situation had left me profoundly saddened, touched in some sore and sensitive places that burned and stung and made me all too aware of my own misgivings about the past and shortcomings in the present. Perhaps I could make some progress on the future. Maybe it wasn't too late for that.

The second package was much larger, but elicited much the same initial response as the first one. It was a flat, rectangular parcel, wrapped in brown paper and delivered by U.P.S. I opened it carefully while Janette looked on. As the paper came away, my smile grew wider. It was the painting I had admired in Penny's apartment. A naked Barb stared down at me from the canvas, ice tongs and empty glass in hand. Cheers.

There was a note stapled to the back of the stretcher frame. It read: "Merry Christmas, with Love, Penny." Next to where the note was attached was a title, newly scrawled on the wood in dark pencil. "Our Lady of Divine Providence, P.S.R., 1986." I chuckled to myself. Divine Providence, indeed.

THE END